D0788977

Evelyn Waugh
and the Problem of Evil

by the same author

Dryden
The Teaching of George Eliot
Milton and Free Will: An Essay in Criticism and Philosophy

Evelyn Waugh
and the Problem of Evil

WILLIAM MYERS

faber and faber
LONDON · BOSTON

First published in 1991
by Faber and Faber Limited
3 Queen Square London WC1N 3AU

Phototypeset by Wilmaset, Birkenhead, Wirral
Printed in Great Britain by
Clays Ltd, St Ives plc

A CIP record for this book is available
from the British Library

ISBN 0–571–14094–7

For David

Contents

Preface

This introduction to the novels of Evelyn Waugh attempts what even he recognized as an old-fashioned task. Reviewing a volume of Orwell's essays, he noted that what he called the new criticism had abandoned 'the hierarchic principle':

It has hitherto been assumed that works of art exist in an order of precedence with the great masters, Virgil, Dante and their fellows, at the top and the popular novel of the season at the bottom. The critic's task has been primarily to preserve and adjust this classification. Their recreation has been to 'discover' recondite work and compete in securing honours each for his own protégé. (*The Essays, Articles and Reviews of Evelyn Waugh*, 1983, p. 305)

I have not thought of Waugh's works as my protégés in writing this book. Nevertheless it is an attempt to secure honours for him as a writer which he has perhaps been denied up to now, to place his novels high in the catalogue of great fiction, and to claim for them an intellectual coherence, subtlety and seriousness which his disconcerting comic gifts and extravagant public and writing persona have tended to put in the shade.

At the same time it also attempts to undertake what Waugh perceived as the work of 'the new critics' who

begin their inquiry into a work of art by asking: 'What kind of man wrote or painted this? What were his motives, conscious or unconscious? What sort of people like his work? Why?'

In Waugh's case, however, the distinction between traditional and later criticism is unreal, since the first task implies the second. His claim to be placed among the canonical writers of 'literature' consists precisely in his manipulations of the people who liked his work or loathed it, and in his projection before a fascinated public of a persona which invites the questions: what kind of man wrote this? what were his motives, conscious or unconscious? In this, as in many other respects, he has remarkable affinities with Dickens.

Waugh's comic gift is what makes his books great. I have on the whole evaded the difficult task of discussing it – I simply assume that his readers read his books and return to them because they enjoy being reduced to helpless and astonished laughter. What I have attempted is the simpler task of exploring the view of people and history in the novels which somehow survives that laughter though often apparently threatened by it. I believe that Waugh's sense of the human person and of divine Providence are irreducibly present in his work, but that what he affirms about them can only be adequately understood in the context of the actual phase of world history in which his books are set (the closing years of the age of Imperialism) and the actual form of the religious convictions (anti-Modernist Catholicism) which enabled him to cope with the evil of those times. Both Imperialist ideology and the world-view which dominated Catholic thinking between 1870 and 1960 have now passed into history and can only be recovered with difficulty. They generated points of view which were then acceptable but which seem to many people now either silly or wicked. I find some of them so myself, but I have not intruded my own views into this book. It seemed to me more useful to establish as accurately as I could the substance of Waugh's thinking and the circumstances that gave rise to it, and to leave the reader to decide how far to consent to his ideas, to condone them, or to condemn them.

In so far as I do address the nature of Waugh's comic writing it is in relation to a concept of Evil which I have borrowed from the French critic Georges Bataille. This is the only overtly 'theoretical' element in this book, and as such may appear out of place. It seemed to me, however, a convenient and not too esoteric way of dealing with the most troubling and exciting aspect of Waugh's work – its sadism, its gleeful, childish irresponsibility, its fascination with lunacy and death. I believe Waugh's engagement with the problem of Evil in this special sense illuminates his treatment of the problem as it is more generally understood, namely the Christian God's tolerance of, and apparent responsibility for, the wretchedness of so much of the human condition. It is not just as a Catholic moralist, but as a Catholic visionary, that Waugh must finally be judged.

This is a short and limited study of Waugh's novels. I hope that before long someone else will write a bigger book on Waugh, covering his travel writing, essays, diaries and letters as well as all the fiction, with the fullness they deserve. It may well prove that Waugh will survive, as Byron has done, because the informal writings are at least as brilliant as the formal ones. I also think that the novels would bear the full weight of theoretical scrutiny, with surprising and fruitful results for theory.

In spite of its modest length and relatively straightforward aims, this book would have contained numerous egregious errors, confused arguments and stylistic infelicities but for the scrupulous attention given to an earlier draft by my colleague, Martin Stannard, the first volume of whose distinguished biography of Waugh was my *vade mecum* in writing about Waugh's life and works up to 1939. I am also very grateful to The Right Revd Mgr Ralph Brown for directing my attention to a crucial reference. Any surviving errors in the text are due entirely to my own carelessness. Quotations are from the current Penguin Books editions of Waugh's novels, his biography of Edmund Campion, and the edition of his letters edited by Mark Amory. All quotations from *Brideshead Revisited*, however, are from the 1951 Penguin edition. I have preferred the original Penguin printing of the novels in the *Sword of Honour* trilogy to the single volume published by Penguin Books under that title, which is not in fact a reprint of the revised 1965 edition published by Chapman and Hall, but a republication of the novels in their original form. I quote from the first edition of Waugh's other works.

CHAPTER ONE

Vorticists:
Decline and Fall and *Vile Bodies*

On 18 April 1926 Evelyn Waugh wrote in his diary:

> I suppose that the desire to merge one's individual destiny in forces outside oneself, which seems to me deeply rooted in most people and shows itself in social service and mysticism and in some manner in debauchery, is really only a consciousness that this is already the real mechanism of life which requires so much concentration to perceive that one wishes to objectify it in more immediate (and themselves subordinate) forces. How badly I write when there is no audience to arrange my thoughts for. (*The Diaries of Evelyn Waugh*, 1983, pp. 250–51)

He was twenty-two and would not hold these views for long, but they are worth quoting because they illustrate the intellectual muddle in which he found himself as a young man, and his dependence as a writer on an audience.

His life was in no less of a muddle. The son of a publisher, Arthur Waugh, he was brought up in prosperous, middle-class circumstances. His elder brother, Alec, had been expelled from Sherborne School and had published a novel about public-school homosexuality. Evelyn was therefore sent to Lancing College, where he made some lasting friendships and received a traditional classical and High Anglican education. He became an agnostic when he was sixteen. More surprisingly he was encouraged to learn drawing and calligraphy. He won a scholarship to Oxford, and initially lived quite soberly. However he soon joined a socially glamorous set, and embarked on a life of drunkenness and romantic homosexual liaisons, his most important relationship at Oxford being with Alastair Graham. He was also closely associated with Harold (later

Sir Harold) Acton, the son of a Florentine art dealer and a wealthy American. Mannered and worldly-wise, Acton was an aesthete and an admirer of Chekhov, T. S. Eliot, Gertrude Stein and Ezra Pound. Other important friends (at a somewhat later date) were the Plunket-Greene family, liberal Catholics, not noted for abstemious living. Waugh was for a time attached to Olivia Plunket-Greene. In one sense these friends did Waugh no good. They encouraged him to merge his individual destiny with something outside himself by drinking too much and getting into debt, and he found himself often enough witnessing scenes of 'cruel' and 'obscene' debauchery and going alone to his bed 'with rather a heavy heart' (*Diaries*, p. 208). Nevertheless, the friendships of these prodigal years were among the most valuable of his life. They gave him an audience to arrange his thoughts for when he began writing.

In 1924 he left Oxford in debt and without a degree and found himself a job in a Welsh preparatory school, Arnold House, which he loathed. He even attempted suicide by swimming out to sea, but he headed into a shoal of jellyfish and retreated to the shore and his clothes. He consoled himself by observing a fellow master who had an insatiable appetite for the boys in his care, and had been precipitately dismissed from four previous schools for sodomy and drunkenness. 'And yet,' Waugh noted, 'he goes on getting better and better jobs without difficulty. It is all very like Bruce and the spider' (*Diaries*, p. 213). In that final sentence there is the seed of the celebrated characterization of Captain Grimes in *Decline and Fall* (1928), and a more general indication of Waugh's delight in the disorder generated by naïvely dedicated recidivists. He tried writing a novel, hopes of becoming secretary to Charles Scott-Moncrieff fell through, and there seemed little chance of his profitably developing his interest in carpentry and draughtsmanship. So he went to Aston Clinton School in Berkshire, where he could more easily keep in touch with his friends. He wrote a short story, 'The Balance', and an essay on the Pre-Raphaelites. The summer of 1926 was spent in the company of Alastair Graham (now a Catholic convert) – Waugh did not get on well with Graham's masterful mother – and at Christmas he was able to visit Graham in Athens, but found the presence of male prostitutes in the flat Graham shared with an attaché from the

British Embassy distasteful. Perhaps the most significant event in his time at Aston Clinton was the attachment he formed with two boys, Charles and Edmund, the development of which is sketched in a series of diary entries, the most striking of which reads:

On Monday afternoon I found Edmund out of bounds and beat him with mixed feelings and an ash plant. He was very sweet and brave about it all. I gave him a Sulka tie as recompense. (*Diaries*, p. 254)

This may be the kernel of the relationship between Paul Penny-feather and Peter Beste-Chetwynde in *Decline and Fall*. In February 1927, Waugh was sacked, possibly for making advances to the matron. He thought of becoming a parson; he accompanied his friends to jazz sessions given by fashionable black musicians, and worked briefly first in a state school, then as a gossip columnist on the *Daily Express*. Finally, through the good offices of a friend, the novelist Anthony Powell, he was invited to write a book on Dante Gabriel Rossetti. He also met the woman who was to be his first wife, The Hon. Evelyn Gardner. On 1 July 1927 he started work on the Rossetti book, and on 3 September he began *Decline and Fall*. *Rossetti, His Life and Works* was published in April 1928 and was well received. Naturally Waugh was pleased but he was taking far greater pleasure in his novel and his engagement.

For a young woman of the period Evelyn Gardner lived a remarkably free and independent life. She shared a flat with a friend, Pansy Pakenham, which was a centre of stylish upper-class bohe-mianism. Waugh was taking a carpentry course, still hoping for the life of an artist-craftsman. When he proposed on Monday 12 December 1927 over dinner in the Ritz Grill, he apparently suggested that 'they should get married "and see how it goes" ' (*Diaries*, p. 305). He was accepted next day over the phone. The match was bitterly opposed by Evelyn Gardner's mother, Lady Burghclere. Nevertheless, the two Evelyns were married on 27 June 1928. Waugh's mildly exaggerated diary entry reads:

A woman was typewriting on the altar. Harold [Acton] best man. Robert Byron gave away the bride, Alec and Pansy the witnesses. Evelyn wore a new black and yellow jumper suit with scarf. (*Diaries*, p. 295)

On 6 July he recorded the end of their honeymoon, his writing to
Lady Burghclere announcing the marriage – she was 'quite inex-
pressibly pained' – and the fact that he had spent Saturday 30 June
'hard at work on the proofs of *Decline and Fall*'.

Both *Rossetti* and *Decline and Fall* express smartly up-to-date
attitudes and yet disclose an unfashionable delight in things Victorian. In *Rossetti* Waugh notes Picasso's 'pelucid excellencies' (p. 14) –
this was a topic on which he was to change his mind – and Rossetti's
lack of interest in 'the necessary relation of forms' (p. 223); yet he
also found meticulously realistic Pre-Raphaelite narrative painting
inexplicably engaging and was fascinated by Rossetti's dependence
on inspiration and his lack of artistic discipline. As a writer of
fiction, Waugh worked like the modern craftsman-designer he had
hoped to be. An important influence on his technique was film. At
Oxford he had written about film editing; the main part of 'The
Balance' has the form of a film scenario, and *Decline and Fall* is 'cut'
like a talkie, particularly the cross-cutting in the Prelude between
Paul's encounter with the drunken Bollinger hearties and the
trembling and excited dons.

Another source of Waugh's sense of form was carpentry. In one of
his later travel books, *Ninety-Two Days* (1934), he was to compare
a carpenter's itch to work on 'a piece of rough timber' with the
writer's desire to take 'the amorphous, haphazard condition in
which life presents' an experience, and put it 'into communicable
form' (p. 13). *Decline and Fall* is shaped in just this way. It begins
and ends with the Bollinger Club in full cry and an encounter
between Paul and one of its leading lights. The symmetry is off-set by
some well-judged contrasts: an inhibited, respectable young man
when the novel begins, and 'consumedly shy of drunkards' (p. 12),
Paul, in his final scene, converses amiably and wisely with his
drunken former pupil, Peter Beste-Chetwynde, now the Earl of
Pastmaster, intelligent and worldly but vulnerable, so different from
the handsome, decent but not very bright Alastair Digby-Vane-
Trumpington of the Prelude. Alastair has meanwhile replaced Paul
as Margot Beste-Chetwynde's lover. The entire novel is similarly

constructed of interlocking sequences of incident and dialogue, with minor characters and recurring motifs giving as much prominence to design as to event, theme and character. One of its lasting pleasures is its marginal narratives, notably the laconic asides from the narrator and the unfeeling Lady Circumference about the death of her son, Little Lord Tangent. Other equally economical and rather more discreet narratives follow the progress of Grimes's implied affair with Clutterbuck, and the career in prostitution of the first Mrs Grimes.

But film and carpentry were not the only contemporary influences on *Decline and Fall*; under Acton's influence, T. S. Eliot was another. From Eliot, Waugh learned to make a collage of brief scenes and snatches of conversation and to 'do' his scenes in different voices. (*He Do the Police in Different Voices* had been a working title for *The Waste Land*.) Waugh had a fine ear for 'voices' – the complacent grandeur of Dr Fagan, '. . . We schoolmasters must temper discretion with deceit. There, I fancy I have said something for you to think about. Good night' (p. 24); the casual aplomb of the young Peter, '. . . Philbrick . . . why haven't you given Mr Pennyfeather a napkin . . . The man's all right, really . . . only he wants watching' (p. 25); and the aristocratic robustness of Lady Circumference, 'So you're the Doctor's hired assassin, eh? Well, I hope you keep a firm hand on my toad of a son . . .' (p. 67). At the other extreme are the ludicrous locutions of the Welsh bandsmen, Philbrick's mock-cockney, and the vulgarity of Flossie Fagan and the newly rich Clutterbucks. These 'voices' enable Waugh to exhibit the absurdity and cruelty of the English class system. He delights in both the self-deceptions disclosed by cliché and the human dislocations implicit in linguistic impropriety. The pomposity of Potts, the fluent hypocrisy of the judicial rhetoric at Paul's trial, and the smug jargon of Sir Wilfred Lucas-Dockery, are examples of the former, Grimes a particularly rich source of the latter. Grimes has never mastered the dialect of the adult tribe; he speaks like a schoolboy: 'The last chap who put me on my feet said I was "singularly in harmony with the primitive promptings of humanity". I've remembered that phrase because somehow it seemed to fit me. Here comes the old man. This is where we stand up' (p. 34). On occasion, however, his conversation rises absurdly to biblical magniloquence:

'. . . Who shall pity me in that dark declivity to which my steps inevitably seem to tend? I have boasted in my youth and held my head high and gone on my way careless of consequences, but ever behind me, unseen, stood stark Justice with his two-edged Sword.' (p. 102)

As in *The Waste Land*, this play of voices is controlled by a presiding voice which combines studied neutrality with a calculated disruption of linguistic expectations. Eliot writes:

> When lovely woman stoops to folly and
> Paces about her room again, alone,
> She smooths her hair with automatic hand,
> And puts a record on the gramophone.
> (*The Waste Land*, lines 253–6)

A comparable feeling for the disjunction between traditional and modern contexts informs the description of Margot recovering from her period and a few days of drug-induced sedation:

As the last of the guests departed Mrs Beste-Chetwynde reappeared from her little bout of veronal, fresh and exquisite as a seventeenth-century lyric. The meadow of green glass seemed to burst into flower under her feet as she passed from the lift to the cocktail table. (p. 133)

Just as Eliot echoes Goldsmith, so Waugh echoes, not a seventeenth-century lyric, but the last stanza of Part One of Tennyson's *Maud*. The presiding authorial voice also controls the stylish eroticism of the world into which Paul is introduced in Part Two. Here, in accents drawn from the works of Ronald Firbank as well as the Decadent prose of the 1890s, Waugh flicks aside the hypocrisies and prudery of the English middle class. As a boy he had been attracted by the drawings of Aubrey Beardsley, and Paul's introduction to King's Thursday reads like a discreet reworking of Beardsley's erotic fantasy *Under the Hill*, in which Wagner's Tannhäuser is entertained in an exquisitely sophisticated and degenerate Venusberg.

But if Waugh's first novel is remarkable for its cool modernity, it also echoes the verbally lush places and extravagant melodrama of the Victorian novel, especially Dickens – whom Waugh included among 'the most daemonic of the masters' (*The Ordeal of Gilbert Pinfold*, 1957, p. 10). Llanabba Castle owes a lot to *Nicholas Nickleby*. Dr Fagan is no Mr Squeers, but Flossie has the libido and vulgarity of his daughter:

> 'Pleased to meet you,' said Miss Fagan. 'Now what I always tell the young chaps as comes here is, "Don't let the dad overwork you." He's a regular Tartar, is Dad, but then you know what scholars are – inhuman. Ain't you,' said Miss Fagan, turning on her father with sudden ferocity – 'ain't you inhuman?' (pp. 23–4)

Equally Dickensian and daemonic are Philbrick's mad confessions, and the convict scenes on Egdon Heath, itself an allusion to Hardy's Wessex, while Lady Circumference is straight out of Thackeray.

This attachment to a well-upholstered, slightly mad Victorianism distinguishes Waugh from contemporaries such as Aldous Huxley. He is in touch with traditions which put modernity into perspective, hence his satire of a merely fashionable aesthetic. Davy Lennox's 'two eloquent photographs of the back of [Margot's] head and one of the reflection of her hands in a bowl of ink' (p. 150) and the amazing décor of King's Thursday point to the danger lurking in Professor Silenus's modernist programme – 'the elimination of the human element from the consideration of form' (p. 120). Silenus presumably wishes art to be no more than a self-referential system of signs. He would like us to look at chairs without ever thinking of them as resting places for bottoms. He would like us to read stories and look at pictures without ever reacting to the situations and characters they depict as if they were real or feeling emotionally involved and morally at risk in our experience of them. He would reject the notion of intelligent readers finding a novel cruel or obscene and closing it with a heavy heart.

There are analogous dangers in the emancipations of Society, and Waugh reminds us, therefore, of the more traditional world represented in the novels of James, Forster and Woolf, in which 'an intelligent, well-educated, well-conducted young man . . . might be expected to acquit himself with decision and decorum in all the emergencies of civilized life' (p. 122). Paul may become a mere shadow when he leaves this world, but only because we are all shadows in our daydreams. *Decline and Fall* is ultimately a fantasy of social and sexual initiation which returns its well-conducted fantasist safely to his own world. Thus even if Paul is not a 'character', he is one of the means by which the human element remains a part of Waugh's design.

As a fantasy, however, *Decline and Fall* never aspires to the status of a full-blown satire. There is no need to draw important conclusions, for example, from Mr Prendergast's discovery '*that there is a species of person called a "Modern Churchman" who draws the full salary of a beneficed clergyman and need not commit himself to any religious belief*' (p. 141), or from the intellectual pretensions of Sir Wilfred Lucas-Dockery. Not even Silenus's disquisition on the Wheel in Luna Park should be read for its message. He categorizes people as either 'static' or 'dynamic' (p. 209), and apparently includes Paul among the former and characters like Grimes, Margot and Alastair among the latter. Earlier, however, he identified the human element his art was supposed to eliminate not with '*being*' but with 'the vile *becoming*' (p. 121). (Waugh's interest in this much-used philosophical distinction derives apparently from his reading of Oswald Spengler [Stannard, p. 170].) Silenus, it seems, like Wittgenstein, whom he so strikingly resembles, changes his mind, but little importance attaches to this, since he dismisses his own philosophizings as 'boring and futile' (p. 209), and the Great Wheel analogy as a mere cinematic conceit. If any broader view emerges from his meditations it is that neither 'being' nor 'becoming' sustain the human element, and that the wisest course is to recognize the distinction and identify with neither.

But if *Decline and Fall* is a fantasy for respectable young men, it is also an entertainment for disreputable ones. This brings us back to Waugh's need of an audience 'to arrange his thoughts for'. It was his consciousness of a secretly inscribed audience with whom he could communicate in an intimate and coded manner that enabled him to write so well in *Decline and Fall*. At one level this intimacy was signalled in a series of private jokes. A number of characters, such as

'David Lennox' and 'Jack Spire' were readily recognizable public figures [Stannard, p. 161], but others were not. Waugh uses the name of his much disliked former Oxford Tutor, C. R. M. F. Cruttwell, for example, in one of Philbrick's stories of low-class criminality, and he portrays Alastair Graham's mother in Lady Circumference. More generally the novel flaunts the emancipated attitudes to sex, race and class which Waugh shared with his friends. As a celebration of the taboo-breaking of a young, intelligent, urbane coterie, *Decline and Fall* is an almost wholly joyful book, which may be why Waugh held it in such affection.

The nature of this taboo-breaking is complex. As we have seen, the play of voices and linguistic modes in *Decline and Fall* is rich and formally elaborate. Waugh introduces a linguistic register such as Grimes's schoolboy-ese and brilliantly overplays it, runs it against the pomposities of Dr Fagan, or suddenly infuses it with the passion of the Psalmist. If the life-force is anywhere in the novel it is in the limitless 'becoming' of its language by which, for example, after Grimes's death, Walter Pater's celebrated meditation on the Mona Lisa is linked to Bergson's notion of the life-force and travestied in Paul's mind and Waugh's prose. But, as Waugh's satire of Silenus's theory of art suggests, there is a second way of attending to this or any other novel, and that is to react to its human elements. Read in this way, *Decline and Fall* is frequently shocking and even unpleasant. And though these two ways of attending to the text are mutually incompatible, attention can shift between them and it is this third position – accepting the formal and the human as distinct but equally valid levels of significance – which Waugh challenges his readers, his intimates on the one hand, and the general reader on the other, to adopt if they can.

It is an essential aspect of the novel's procedures, therefore, that its treatment of sexuality, race and class should be radically inconsistent. The cruel homophobia in the presentation of Miles Malpractice and Lord Parakeet, for example, is set beside a celebration of Peter's pubescent seductiveness, yet the novel's homophobia and its homoeroticism are equally stylish. The challenge is to acknowledge the latter whatever one's reactions to the former (anger on behalf of Miles, disgust at Silenus's appraisal of

Peter's skin). More disturbing is Waugh's blasé attitude to race, his far from neutral use of the word 'nigger' and the offensive representation of Margot's lover, Chokey. Yet even here a subtle game is being played. At the level of 'life', we are being challenged to place *ourselves* in relation to Chokey – among the sophisticates who take his role as Margot's lover with casual amusement, or among the lubricious like Colonel Sidebotham and the Clutterbucks who fantasize about savage slayings and *'uncontrollable passions*. See what I mean?' (p. 78). At the level of form, however, the play of voices – Margot's, Chokey's and the leering young Clutterbuck's – is just mischievously brilliant.

These two ways of attending to the 'racialism' in the novel are most clearly in evidence in its treatment of the Welsh:

'The Welsh character is an interesting study,' said Dr Fagan. '. . . From the earliest times the Welsh have been looked upon as an unclean people. It is thus that they have preserved their racial integrity. Their sons and daughters rarely mate with human-kind except their own blood-relations.' (p. 65–6)

At a period when the question of 'racial integrity' was regarded as a serious intellectual issue, this functions self-evidently as parody. In describing the Silver Band in flagrantly offensive language – 'they halted and edged back, those behind squinting and moulting over their companions' shoulders' (ibid.) – Waugh is ridiculing all respectable verbal timidities. There are thus two opposed sets of readers inscribed in the text; the taboo-breakers who enjoy the verbal game and the taboo-bound who cannot distinguish between signifiers and what they signify.

The third area of taboo-breaking in the novel is class, in which the problems of sex and race are also involved. (Part of Peter's charm is his combination of snobbery, sexual sophistication and virginal innocence.) Again, the reader's capacity to engage with both kinds of attending is put on trial. Do we despise or relish the vulgarities of the Clutterbucks and the Fagan sisters? Is it snobbery or appreciation of the author's stylistic verve which enables us to relish the Bollinger Club, with its 'epileptic royalty . . . uncouth peers . . . smooth young men of uncertain tastes from embassies and

legations; illiterate lairds . . . ambitious young barristers and Conservative candidates' (p. 9), who stoned a fox with champagne
bottles at their last meeting? Do we resist the lure of Margot and her
wealth, and if not, is it her exquisite eroticism which bewitches us or
Waugh's elegant prose? Grimes is a key figure here. After his
marriage he tells Paul about the miseries of being Dr Fagan's son-in-
law:

'. . . It's not Flossie, mind . . . In a way I've got quite to like her. She likes
me, anyway, and that's the great thing. The Doctor's my trouble . . . Always
laughing at me in a nasty kind of way and making me feel small. You know
the way Lady Circumference talks to the Clutterbucks – like that . . .'
(p. 109)

Flossie did warn us. But how does Grimes's lament reflect on any
reactions *we* may have had to the Clutterbucks' racialism on the one
hand, or their vulgarity on the other? The novel's virtuoso display of
social and literary usage may signal its author's familiarity with his
more emancipated and worldly audience, but it does not unconditionally adopt their point of view. Important things about 'life' can
be uttered in Grimes's childish slang, and this gives the text a vital
independence from the perspectives of its more sophisticated
readers.

Literary hedonism and the human element are thus in complex
tension in *Decline and Fall*. But a reading of the novel which moves
freely between them discloses a significant connection. Both the
formal play of the novel's various voices and 'life' as it is lived in
Margot's world are based on an assumption of invulnerability, of
imperviousness to change. It is this quality in the *form* of the novel
which, for example, makes the death of Mr Prendergast acceptable –
there can be no real pain in so mannered a text – and the same
quality informs the mannered lives of Margot and Peter. They are
almost incestuously united in maintaining the illusion that their
wealth and privilege are natural and safe.

In this respect they are different from other 'dynamic' characters.
Grimes, Dr Fagan and Alastair never experience any anxiety about
the permanence of their worlds. For the Beste-Chetwyndes, however, imperviousness to vicissitude depends on an act of the will and,

in Peter's case, on loyalty also. His vulnerability is consequently more obvious than Margot's. It acts as a check on, and rebuke to, her eroticism and her cool command of upper-class speech and the market economy. It is only through him, therefore, that *her* vulnerability becomes apparent. Her self-concern is only shameful on Peter's account – hence her need for him to approve of her lovers, and his readiness to do so. Momentarily they find a fragile resolution of these tensions in her decision to marry Paul to whom they are both attracted. But their fantasy, unlike Paul's, is not under control, and its collapse is humiliating. One of the novel's finest touches is the description of Peter when Paul is arrested:

> Sir Alastair's amiable pink face gaped in blank astonishment. 'Good God,' he said, 'how damned funny! At least it would be at any other time.' But Peter, deadly white, had left the restaurant. (p. 158)

More drawn-out but quite as fine is the shameful yet touching scene in prison when Margot tells Paul that she is not going to wait for him, especially because we know that Paul himself is thinking about how Margot will be in ten years' time. Peter's final scene with Paul brings these matters to their sad conclusion. He is upset by his mother's marriage to the recently ennobled Lord Metroland. 'You know you ought never to have got mixed up with me and Metroland,' he tells Paul (Epilogue). It is distressing to find him referring to Margot so crudely.

The novel's dream of a changeless world of amoral privilege and freedom is thus subtly placed through Peter and Margot as well as through Grimes and Flossie. So presumably are any of its readers who have indulged in its brilliant surface and morally value-free organization and not recognized that surfaces can conceal the most sensitive adjustments of the will. This is implicit in the two Bollinger dinners with which the novel begins and ends. Alastair in the first is amiable, blundering and naïve, Peter in the second worldly, sensitive, and miserable. Each suggests that the motives underlying debauchery may not always be the obvious ones. Peter's ruminative sadness in particular touches us with a sense of what it might mean to be brought up in a world predicated on changelessness and then to lose it. As a result the novel's elegant urbanity moves decisively away from cynicism and towards compassion.

Waugh finished his second novel, *Vile Bodies* (1930), just over a year after the publication of *Decline and Fall*. It had been a bad year. Shortly after the wedding his wife became ill. She recovered and they went on a cruise. She again fell ill, needed an operation, and at one point was thought to be dying but was eventually well enough for them to tour extensively in the Mediterranean. They spent too much money. On their return, Waugh retired to the country to write a novel about a young writer desperately short of money. He wrote quickly but felt 'chained to [the] novel . . . It [was] a welter of sex and snobbery, written simply in the hope of selling some copies' (*The Letters of Evelyn Waugh*, 1980, p. 37). His wife stayed in London with a friend, Nancy Mitford, and went to parties like the ones he was writing about in his novel, often escorted by an attractive Old Etonian, John Heygate. Waugh approved of the arrangement. However on 9 July he received a letter from Evelyn to say that she and Heygate had fallen in love. He returned to London, but reconciliation proved impossible. Getting back to *Vile Bodies* was appallingly difficult. He retreated to the country, then to Ireland as the guest of Nancy Mitford's sister, Diana, and her husband, Bryan Guinness. He went to motor races in Belfast – they were to feature in his novel to which he had at last returned but found 'infinitely difficult . . . It all seems to shrivel up & rot internally and I am relying on a sort of cumulative futility for any effect it may have' (*Letters*, p. 39). It was, however, the commercial success he wanted. The divorce decree was granted three days before its publication, in January 1930.

   After such disasters, it is not surprising that *Vile Bodies* is an uneven production. In a brilliant analysis of the typescript, Stannard has established that the section of the novel written before the collapse of Waugh's marriage ends 'almost exactly in the middle, at the end of Chapter Six' (Stannard, p. 206). Those first six chapters are among the funniest in English fiction. They open with the well-established device of a sea voyage for which there is a Dickensian precedent in *Little Dorrit*. This enables Waugh to establish more broadly based social relationships than we find in *Decline and Fall*. Through Mr Outrage and Father Rothschild we are in touch with politics, through Mrs Melrose Ape with religion and the press, through Adam Fenwyck-Symes with publishing, through Lady Throbbing, Mrs Blackwater and Agatha Runcible with Society, and through the ship's officers, commercial travellers and customs men with the coarse accents of English popular culture. A second, equally venerable device, that of the inn or hotel – in this case Waugh's portrait of the Cavendish Hotel and its proprietress, Rosa Lewis, thinly disguised as Shepheard's Hotel and Lottie Crump – keeps these characters in touch with one another and further extends the novel's range. Finally there is the thoroughly Victorian device of the party – or rather parties. The scope of the subject matter, the numbers of the characters and the movement between them matches similar compositions by Dickens, but the pace is swifter, the drawing lighter. The first four chapters, for example, are constructed round the secret that shy Miss Brown, who urges the Bright Young Things to come to her house, is the Prime Minister's daughter, a detail disclosed to the reader (and the exotically dressed Agatha Runcible) at the Prime Ministerial breakfast table. Equally expert is the cutting between the actual party for Mrs Melrose Ape given by Margot Metroland (which Lady Circumference ruins) and the libellous fantasy of the banned gossip-columnist, Simon Balcairn, immediately before his suicide.

After Chapter Six, however, there are significant changes of tone and plotting. What had been hectic and irresponsible becomes frenetic and cruel. The second half of the novel is not so much about sex and snobbery as about booze and money. Nina betrays Adam because Ginger is rich. The focus of the action narrows to the concerns of three people and it moves away from London to the Blount film-making episodes and the motor races. There are also some loose ends and badly conceived ideas in the second half of the novel. Waugh himself recognized that the monologue of the middle-aged woman in the train (pp. 137–40) – imitating the pub monologue in *The Waste Land* – and the inept film about John Wesley being made at the home of Colonel Blount were too drawn out (Julian Jebb, *Writers at Work*, 1968, pp. 108–9). But the novel's most unsatisfactory element is the ending: the war is a mere expedient for winding up a narrative that is out of control. Waugh told Henry Yorke (the novelist, Henry Green) that he would stop writing as soon as he had 'enough pages covered to call it a book' (*Letters*, p. 39). He was never again to drive a novel out of history as he does here; for a writer who was to develop so keen an historical sense, such a move signalled a loss of imaginative energy. It was also a careless move. Waugh re-introduces many of his favourite characters from *Decline and Fall* into his second novel. His invented war would have to be ignored if, like Thackeray, he were to do the same in later novels.

But there is a more deep-seated failure, which becomes evident in the descriptions of the two parties in Chapter Eight, the Airship Party and the party at Anchorage House. The Airship Party is a failure for everyone but Mary Mouse, who makes love on deck with the Maharajah of Pukkapore, and Margot Metroland, who slips away to it for an assignation with Alastair Trumpington. The party at Anchorage House is the party Margot slips away from. We are introduced to it through the excited historical vision of Mrs Hoop. It is a party largely for people of a kind we have not met before, 'pious and honourable people . . . who had represented their country in foreign places and sent their sons to die for her in battle, people of decent and temperate life, uncultured, unaffected, unembarrassed, unassuming, unambitious people', a cut above Paul Pennyfeather's family perhaps, but not the emancipated socialites nor the domineering grandees of Waugh's best comic writing. After the parenthesis about 'vile bodies' at the Airship Party, the introduction of these people suggests that an important comparison is about to be developed, but it isn't. Instead we are given a detachable short story concerning the rejection of Edward Throbbing by the dowdy daughter of the Duchess of Stayle, and her mother's refusal to accept that she has done any such thing. The Duchess's complacency might serve to justify the outlook of the degenerates in the dirigible, but the later scene in which Peter Pastmaster swears miserably at his stepfather, Lord Metroland, while both know Alastair is upstairs with Margot, hardly suggests a whole-hearted endorsement of fashionable self-indulgence.

Technically, Chapter Eight is a disaster. Its succession of incidents fails to compose itself into a formally engaging set of contrasts. There can be no play, therefore, between the two kinds of attention – to form and to life – which characterizes an intelligent reading of *Decline and Fall*. This creates a need for expository coherence of the kind Mr Outrage, Father Rothschild and Lord Metroland are searching for in their conversation in Anchorage House. The subject of this conversation is the irresponsibility of the young: 'What does all this stand for,' Lord Metroland asks, 'if there's going to be no one to carry it on?' 'Don't you think,' Rothschild says gently, 'that perhaps it is all in some way historical?' Up to this point, Rothschild has been a comically self-important Machiavell, but the word 'gently' suggests that he is also humane. What he has to say, however, is trivial and confused: the phrase 'in some way' is slack, and his suggestion that 'all these divorces' show 'an almost fatal hunger for permanence' is a sub-Chestertonian paradox that fails to develop the theme introduced at the Airship Party with Adam's suggestion to Nina 'that a marriage ought to *go on* – for quite a long time . . .' (p. 123). Besides, if a hunger for permanence is fatal, what do Lady Anchorage's pious and honourable guests want and think they have got? Father Rothschild also suggests that a central teaching of the Catholic Church is the platitude that 'If a thing's worth doing at all, it's worth doing well', and then that the 'young people have got hold of another end of the stick, and for all we know it may be the right one' (p. 132). This is absurd: Jesuits do not go around declaring that Young People might be right and the Catholic Church might be wrong – at least they did not do so in 1930. The conversation then moves on to the coming war, which no one has bothered to tell Mr Outrage about, and 'a radical instability in our whole world-order' (p. 133). At this point Lord Metroland interjects, 'I don't see how all that explains why my stepson should drink like a fish and go about everwhere with a negress.' 'I think they're connected, you know,' Father Rothschild weakly replies. 'But it's all very difficult.'

The problem with this conversation is that it is tonally inconsistent, like the chapter of which it is a part. Outrage's petulance is mildly funny, but Waugh fails to manage an appropriate transition into the more serious passage about their 'walking into the jaws of destruction again'. This suggests that there may indeed be a connection between 'parties' and 'world war' but the theme is not pursued; war in *Vile Bodies* is finally no more than a cynical way of bringing the story, not the world, to an end. After Chapter Six parts of *Vile Bodies* are, quite simply, badly written. Waugh seems to have lost his sense of an audience while he was writing it, and consequently of a stable position from which to engage with the chaos he depicts. The breakup of his marriage apparently deprived him of the sense that he understood those who understood him. He was particularly upset by the reaction of his homosexual friends to the separation. 'It is extraordinary,' he wrote, 'how homosexual people however kind & intelligent simply don't understand at all what one feels in this kind of case' (*Letters*, p. 40). But did anyone understand – anyone, that is, in the magic circle of privileged readers for whom he thought he had *really* been writing? Perhaps only 'pious and honourable people' understood why marriages ought to last. In which case what would he do for an audience?

The fact remains that Waugh persisted in writing this book, enduring as he did so the formal disintegration of his comic mode and the withering of his collusive understanding with an inscribed readership. In the process, however, he became a moralist. *Decline and Fall* relished ambivalence: the 'inhuman' Dr Fagan was also a wit, Margot both selfish and vulnerable. The combinations were piquant, the reader's sense of form was flattered by them. Even our recognition that Peter's relationship with Margot was flawed left us reassured about our own capacity for discriminating sympathy. This delicately managed play between different modes and levels of 'appreciation' yields to something more explicit and savagely indignant in *Vile Bodies*. Whereas Dr Fagan shared the joke of his own egotism at least with the more intelligent of his victims, Colonel Blount's hugely comic solipsism is crafty and self-absorbed. In *Vile Bodies*, the story of Chastity is told with the same kind of economy as that of the first Mrs Grimes; the bizarre reappearances of the drunken major seem gloriously inconsequential in the main body of the text; but Chastity ends up a bedraggled campfollower and the major ends up fucking her in front of an exhausted Adam. It is a cruel and obscene conclusion.

Disorder in *Vile Bodies* is thus finally a moral matter. Its consequences are represented in the fate of Agatha Runcible. Agatha merges her individual destiny in forces outside herself, possibly because she has no inner self to lose, and because she is always alone. (' "I'm afraid I'm all alone," said Miss Runcible. "Isn't it too shaming" ' – p. 156.) Her desperate career in the racing car and her subsequent nightmares transpose Silenus's image of the Wheel into a less complacent mode. Agatha is a human racing car. Whereas 'mechanical drudges such as Lady Metroland's Hispano Suiza, or Mrs Mouse's Rolls-Royce . . . or the "general reader's" Austin Seven . . . have definite "being" just as much as their occupants' and maintain 'their essential identity to the scrap heap . . . *real* cars, . . . those vital creations of metal who exist solely for their own propulsion through space . . . are in perpetual flux; a vortex of combining and disintegrating units'. As such they 'offer a very happy illustration of the metaphysical distinction between "being" and "becoming"' (p. 161). We do not have to take this facetious metaphysical distinction seriously. Nevertheless the ambivalence about 'being' and 'becoming' in *Decline and Fall* has yielded in *Vile Bodies* to a rejection of the phoney vitalism of 'becoming' in favour of maintaining one's 'essential identity to the scrap heap'. This is what Agatha loses.

But the 'essential identity' most at risk in *Vile Bodies* is Waugh's own. In its second, horrific phase the novel deconstructs the implicit assumptions by which the author's own 'subject-position' was earlier maintained. A lot was therefore at stake in the second half of the novel, and it is Waugh's achievement here, as well as his subsequent religious conversion, which sets the course for all his later fiction. The key to an understanding of that achievement is his treatment of Adam, Nina and Ginger.

Just as the human element is carefully protected in *Decline and Fall*, so each of the three major characters has a humanizing moment of vulnerability in *Vile Bodies* – Adam when he dances in Lady Metroland's hall, 'jigging to himself in simple high spirits' (p. 78); Nina (later in the same chapter) when she makes love for the first time, hates it, tells Adam about the cheque, and finally says, 'It's awful to think that I shall probably never, as long as I live, see you dancing like that again all by yourself' (p. 83); and Ginger when he announces in all innocence at the Airship Party that he has found a pal in Miles Malpractice. But whereas Grimes gives Flossie her due and Peter just manages to keep faith with his mother, the three characters in *Vile Bodies* betray each other pretty thoroughly. Nina marries Ginger for his money, and Ginger and Adam haggle over her price. But there are distinctions to be made even here. Ginger, for example, is not quite the innocent he seems: 'a hundred pounds is the deuce of a lot,' he tells Adam. '. . . And I'm just getting a couple of polo ponies over from Ireland' (p. 196). Perhaps his myopic naïvety has an element of self-knowing craftiness in it: at any rate the values he places on his wife and his horse seem remarkably similar to those of the successful rival in Tennyson's *Locksley Hall*. On the other hand, Nina is less shallow than she likes to appear: there is a touch of shame in her little speeches which qualify the harshest judgement against her. Neither, however, ever acts with full deliberation. They may choose to be less knowing than they could be, but less knowing they certainly are.

Adam, however, has no such excuses. He knows that 'a marriage ought to *go on* – for quite a long time', and that his conversations with Nina are shallow. He also knows why she needs to keep them that way, and what he is about when he seduces her at the Nursing Home Party, beds her at Shepheard's Hotel, and then sells her to Ginger. Perhaps the most chilling moment in the novel occurs at Colonel Blount's pseudo-Dickensian Christmas when (as if she had no more significance than Little Lord Tangent) we learn that Agatha Runcible is dead:

'Did I tell you I went to Agatha's funeral? There was practically no one there except the Chasms and some aunts. I went with Van, rather tight, and got stared at. I think they felt I was partly responsible for the accident . . .'

'What about Miles?'

'He's had to leave the country, didn't you know?'

'Darling, I only came back from my honeymoon to-day. I haven't heard anything . . . You know there seems to be none of us left now except you and me.'

'And Ginger.'
'Yes, and Ginger.' (p. 206)

This is a heavily coded exchange. Miles, the homosexual, has presumably fled from prosecution. But the key words are 'And Ginger'. They tell us that Adam is quite aware of what he is responsible for; he at least never kids himself.

It is a remarkable achievement for Waugh to represent the personal corruption of his victim-hero so laconically. It makes Adam much more interesting than Paul Pennyfeather or Peter Pastmaster. The character whose experience most nearly reflects Waugh's own is the one really guilty character in the novel. He is guilty because he is not deluded. Consequently he is also the one who survives as a person, who maintains his essential identity to the scrap heap. The implicit moral seems to be that the only way to keep one's individual destiny from merging with forces outside oneself is to accept responsibility for the whole of one's life, even the rotten bits. Shortly after finishing *Vile Bodies* Waugh realized that the most accurate and convenient word for responsibility for the rotten bits was 'sin', but even before his conversion he had discovered the authorial subject-position of all his later fiction; from now on he would write as a sinful moralist in a sinful world.

CHAPTER TWO

Barbarians:
Black Mischief,
A Handful of Dust and *Scoop*

Waugh's third book was a mildly fictionalized account of his travels of the previous year. *Labels, A Mediterranean Journey* (1930) represents him as travelling alone, and transfers some of his experiences with Evelyn to an imaginary couple. A prefatory Note announces that since the time of the events which it records, his 'views on several subjects, and particularly on Roman Catholicism, [had] developed and changed' (p. 8). Without, apparently, having undergone any conversion crisis, he had been received into the Catholic Church in September 1930. In gratitude for his conversion he wrote *Edmund Campion: Jesuit and Martyr* (1935), the biography of a Jesuit who was executed by Elizabeth I. It contains some of his clearest statements about Catholicism and history.

He assumed, when he became a Catholic, that his marriage to Evelyn Gardner was binding in the eyes of the Church and that he would be unable to remarry in her lifetime. He faced, therefore, a lonely future. Between 1930 and 1936, he made three journeys to Abyssinia and others to Latin America, Morocco and Europe, writing them up in three books, *Remote People* (1931), *Ninety-Two Days, The Account of a Tropical Journey Through British Guiana and Part of Brazil* and *Waugh in Abyssinia* (1936). Otherwise he lived a rootless, gilded existence. His friendship with the Guinnesses lapsed, but he remained close to Nancy Mitford, and formed a romantic friendship with Lady Diana Cooper, actress, society beauty, and wife of a Conservative politician. His circle of friends now included the Lygon family at whose home, Madresfield Court, he frequently stayed. The Lygons were children of the 7th Earl of Beauchamp who was living abroad because of a homosexual scandal. Waugh was particularly fond of Lady Mary and Lady Dorothy Lygon to whom he wrote a series of amusingly obscene letters as if to children still in the nursery. (He was living a life of calculated promiscuity and serious repentance.) He also fell in love with Teresa Jungman, but she was a Catholic and neither could nor would marry him.

Some time after his conversion, he learned that in Catholic law his marriage was possibly null and void, and in 1933 a Church Court took evidence. Evelyn Nightingale (as Evelyn Gardner became) and Lady Pansy Lamb recall Waugh's pumping them to say that he and Evelyn did not intend having children, which was not true (Stannard, pp. 352–3). If Waugh was in bad faith on this point, he would have been in 'mortal sin' for the rest of his days, living daily with the prospect of damnation. Mrs Nightingale's account of the proceedings, however, is technically inaccurate, and the evidence of Waugh's finding security and consolation in the Church is strong. We must therefore assume that he himself believed in the evidence given to the tribunal. In any case the annulment was granted on the ground that neither party had participated in the wedding ceremony with sufficient seriousness (Stannard, p. 155), which seems likely. The issue is important: at stake is Waugh's integrity as a writer, a matter of less significance to him than the saving of his soul but perhaps not unconnected with it. In 1937 he married Laura Herbert, herself a convert. They settled in the country, and Waugh quickly assumed the persona of a country gentleman. He and Laura travelled to Mexico in 1938 to study the atheistic regime of General Cardenas, which resulted in another travel book, *Robbery Under Law: The Mexican Object-Lesson* (1939).

Religion and travel were thus major determinants of Waugh's thinking in the 1930s. He was instructed in the Catholic faith in the summer of 1930; almost immediately afterwards he went to Abyssinia for the coronation of Ras Tafari as the Emperor Haile Selassie. This double experience gave him a sense of history which was never to alter and which was very much of its time. Waugh's Catholicism was that of a brief and untypical phase of Catholic history which the First Vatican Council initiated and the Second closed. In condemning 'Modernism' in religion, the Church claimed,

notably in the encyclical *Pascendi* (1907), that Christianity had an
intellectual rather than an experiential basis, and emphasized the
importance of submission to the formal declarations of the Church
authorities. The political culture to which Waugh's work alludes
was that of European Imperialism from about 1880 to 1945. The
dialectic in his major works is thus grounded in the incompatible
and equally outdated ideologies of anti-Modernist Catholicism to
which he adhered, and imperialist politics which he found anoma-
lous, but it remains intelligible and important; the issues raised in his
greatest work are humanly significant because they are historical.

The fiction produced in the age of imperialism was neither so
insular nor so optimistic as that of the high Victorian period.
Foreigners were less stereotyped. There was an attempt to represent
Chinese, Indians, Arabs and Africans in their own worlds, by turns
savage, possessed of the ancient wisdom or the ancient terrors of
'primitive' people, or informed with cultural traditions as venerable
as those of Europe. These new perspectives registered a loss of that
confidence in Western religion and science on which the unthinking
imperialism satirized, for example, in E. M. Forster's *A Passage to
India*, was based. The writings of Rudyard Kipling and Joseph
Conrad represent isolated individuals or small groups trying to
survive in distant places without the support of the established
institutions – schools, universities, military academies, the Church,
sometimes even the Law – and the assured structure of class
differences at home. They accordingly stake out new kinds of order,
psychological and political, against a background of incipient
anarchy and personal disintegration. Of pious and honourable
stock, they are typically victims of, or survivivors in, a confusing
cultural relativism. Even the authority of a narrator such as Kipling
himself in the Preface to *Life's Handicap* requires validation by an
Indian story-teller, Gobind, an old man who 'has come to the
turnstiles of Night' and to whom 'all the creeds in the world seem
. . . wonderfully alike and colourless' (1964 edn., p. ix). In Kipling's
'The Bridge-Builders' a senior engineer, Findlayson, is amused to
hear his foreman, Peroo – a widely travelled Lascar from Bulsar and,
like Gobind, a believer in many religions and none – speaking of the
bridge they are building as their joint work; but, supplied by Peroo

with opium to get through the night when the rising Ganges puts the bridge under threat, Findlayson hears Krishna instructing his fellow Hindu Gods about the mutability of all things including themselves. What finally binds Findlayson and Peroo together is a sense of the triviality of the present against the backdrop of history. Only their personal honour has value, which for each of them is no stronger than their bridge, and is therefore extinguishable. The very contingency of honour so understood gives its possessors their only dignity.

The values emerging from these narratives of postponed nihilism – self-control, honour, duty, devotion to tribe or nation – apparently disclose levels of experience that are culturally transcendant, deeply personal, and radically contingent. They do not abolish racial or class differences but make possible a bonding or informal Freemasonry between elect individuals of different races and cultures. (Waugh was to describe Kipling's religion as a 'sinister . . . blend of Judaism, Mithraism and Mumbo-jumbo masonry' (*Essays*, p. 306). The exercise of power thereby becomes an arena of heroic action and the source of important benefits for the non-heroic masses – subject peoples, women, children. But as the final phase of Kipling's career attests, such values and such narratives lost their ideological power when futility could not be effectively postponed. They were in turn evoked, validated and undermined by the experience and the literature of world war. The liberal response to this breakdown is represented in *A Passage to India*, where the failure of Aziz and Fielding to achieve the unity binding Peroo and Findlayson signifies the failure of the imperialist project. Any hope there is in the narrative derives from a return to a belief in progress as a process of gradual enlightenment, blended with an optimistic demythologizing of Hindu ritual as against Kipling's pessimistic one. Forster's project is finally old-fashioned. It was too much like wish-fulfilling sentimentality for Waugh and his generation.

For them the collapse of imperialist ideology made distant places and foreign cultures little more than an arena for the further breaking of taboos. Homosexuality was openly practised in Athens; red-light districts in the Near East were more glamorous than Soho. Waugh freely admitted his fascination with 'distant lands and

barbarous places, and particularly . . . the borderlands of conflict-
ing cultures and states of development' (*Ninety-Two Days*, p. 13).
He was excited by foreign brothels, sexual exhibitionism, slavery,
primitive nudity, and the sexual implications of racial dominance.
But even in *Labels* he was forced to question his own cultural
assumptions. The English historical imagination reduced everything
to an inchoate sense of period: examination of the present –

this absurd little jumble of antagonizing forces, of negro rhythm and
psycho-analysis, of mechanical invention and decaying industry, of infinitely expanding means of communication and infinitely receding substance
of the communicable, of liberty and inertia (p. 40)

– was limited to speculations about 'what . . . the picture of
ourselves in the minds of our descendants' would eventually be. A
more rigorous examination of how things were connected was
required. The West rightly suffered from a 'collective inferiority
complex' (p. 110), and was 'humbled . . . by the many excellencies
of Chinese, Indians, and even savages'. Waugh was contemptuous of
'Mohammedan art, history, scholarship, [and] social, religious,
[and] political organisation' (pp. 110–11), but he found 'the
wrangling and resentment of northern slums' (p. 86) compared
poorly with the 'intensely human joviality and inquisitiveness' of the
Arabs of Port Said, who impressed him with 'their animal-like
capacity for curling up and sleeping in the dust, their unembarrassed
religious observances, their courtesy to strangers, their uncontrolled
fecundity, the dignity of their old men'.

The stance has obvious affinities with Kipling's. Like Kipling,
Waugh believed 'in government . . . that there is no form of
government ordained from God . . . that the anarchic elements in
society are so strong that it is a whole-time task to keep the peace'
(*Robbery under Law*, pp. 16–17). A conservative had

positive work to do . . . Barbarism is never finally defeated; given propitious
circumstances, men and women will commit every conceivable atrocity. The
danger does not come merely from habitual hooligans; we are all potential
recruits for anarchy . . . Once the prisons of the mind have been opened, the
orgy is on. (*Robbery under Law*, pp. 278–9)

Societies and individuals alike were thus threatened by the orgiastic, the primitive and the irrational, in their own minds as well as among remote people. This too smacks of Kipling. Unlike Kipling, however, Waugh believed that he had a better resource for resisting atrocity than heroic self-control, namely the dispensations of the Catholic Church.

The temper of his new religion is exactly expressed in *The Belief of Catholics* (1927) by Ronald Knox, a brilliant Anglican convert, by then a Catholic priest, whom Waugh met while writing *Edmund Campion*, and whose friend and biographer he became. Waugh may have read *The Belief of Catholics* while under instruction – he refers to it in *Ronald Knox* (1959) as a 'text-book for countless catechumens' (p. 324) – and in a review in 1944 (*Essays*, pp. 277–80), he summarizes Catholic apologetics with a précis of the arguments advanced in Knox's book. Knox represents the Church as being in many ways an agreeably conservative institution, as 'the repository of long traditions, the undying, unmoved spectator of the thousand phases and fashions that have passed over the world' (p. 32). 'Catholicism,' he writes, 'appeals . . . to the lovers of order. It beckons like a life-boat to the shipwrecked souls who have seen the conventions go down under their feet' (p. 201). Though distrustful of capitalism, the Church rejected state socialism and opposed atheistic communism implacably. It was also an imperialist institution, governed by a Vatican bureaucracy strongly reinforced by the definition in 1870 of papal infallibility. Missionary activity had developed alongside European imperialism. Waugh was continually meeting larger-than-life priests on his travels, establishing their own little patches of ecclesiastical law and order in remote and barbarous places. But unlike the heroes of Conrad and Kipling, these priests claimed to be working for an empire that commanded profounder assent than the provisional pragmatism of beleaguered conservatism, and this claim finally put the Church as deeply at odds with current conservative as with current radical ways of thought.

This can be readily seen in *Edmund Campion*. At one point, Waugh represents Campion as trying to salvage his academic career in the English settlement in Ireland known as the Pale, after his Catholic convictions had forced him to leave Oxford. At first,

Waugh suggests, Campion adopted the uncomplicated imperialistic stance of the other English settlers,

who were confident of their own superiority and the beneficence of their rule; they spoke of the unadministered, alien territories almost exactly as their countertypes, the colonial officials of the nineteenth century, might speak of the bush lands of Africa; they retailed anecdotes of native savagery and superstition, and saw in English education the only cure for them. (p. 36)

In the end, however, Catholicism ranged Campion alongside the 'mere Irish' and against the government of his country. This move, Waugh argues, was grounded in two things, Campion's recognition that 'heresy was a matter of great importance', and his 'love of holiness'. The two went together. Like that other great Catholic convert, John Henry Newman, Waugh believed that religious devotion could only be sustained by the dogmatic principle, by vigorous and intellectually exact beliefs. The spirit of the Elizabethan settlement, however, at least as Waugh represents it, rejected both, substituting intellectual fudge for religious teaching and tepidity for full-hearted devotion. The result was an ethos of compromise and trimming in British political culture generally, and in British conservatism in particular, which Waugh despised and his new religion rejected.

And there was another problem. As we have seen, at the heart of anti-Modernist Catholicism was the assertion that Faith was not primarily experiential but intellectual. This applied particularly to conversion. Knox writes:

Neither the moral effort which submission to the Church involves, nor the grace which is the supernatural coefficient of that effort, carries your reason beyond your premisses. You do not, in becoming a Catholic, commit 'intellectual suicide,' you follow your reason to its legitimate conclusions. (*The Belief of Catholics*, pp. 174–5)

Conversion, in other words, followed a sober weighing of arguments about God's existence and the history of Christianity. Catholic belief was 'based upon an act of private judgment' (p. 45) and Catholic claims, in the first instance, were 'historical statements' (p. 49). It followed that the reasoning which led to faith must be available to all, to the 'mere Irish' or the wrangling and resentful inhabitants of northern slums as well as to the educated and the civilized: 'a glance at the Penny Catechism,' Knox writes, 'would disabuse any unbiassed mind that the Church, even in dealing with simple folk, conceals from them the intellectual basis of their religion' (p. 41). Catholicism thus put all human beings more or less on the same moral and intellectual footing. At 'the root of all Catholic apologetics', Waugh argues in *Edmund Campion*, lies 'the claim . . . that the Faith is . . . completely compelling to *any* who give it an "indifferent and quiet audience" ' (p. 101 – my italics). Knox agreed. In arguments closely related to those advanced by Newman in *An Essay in Aid of A Grammar of Assent*, Knox claims that

there exists among mankind a sort of rough, common-sense metaphysic which demands as its first postulate the existence of a divine principle in things. It can be refined . . . by the philosopher; it is equally valid (we hold) whether as it presents itself to the charcoal-burner or as it presents itself to the sage. (pp. 61–2)

This fundamentally egalitarian principle had serious implications for the conservative. Inequalities 'of wealth and position' may, as Waugh argues in *Robbery Under Law*, be 'inevitable'; men may 'naturally arrange themselves in a system of classes'; and 'such a system' may be 'necessary for any form of co-operative work' (p. 17); but the claim of Catholic teaching to be valid for all times and all peoples was ultimately subversive of the system of differences on which the mere conservative relied. It certainly left no room for pretensions to racial superiority – 'Christianity and the race myth cannot long work together' (*Robbery Under Law*, p. 271) – and it marginalized subtler differences of education, sensibility and even self-command on which English and imperialist ideology relied and to which Waugh himself was unashamedly drawn. His religion thus alienated him from the political, and in the last analysis even from the social culture of the country in which he was born and the class to which he aspired.

His conservative instincts were, however, satisfied by another aspect of Catholic intellectualism. In day-to-day experience authentic religious convictions inevitably consorted in the mind with fancies and guesses that took whatever persuasiveness they had from the surrounding culture. Discriminations between the authentic and the inauthentic in the minds of the faithful, priest and charcoal burner alike, had still to be made. Hence the need for authoritative dogmatic teachings by the Church, and also for sustained intellectual meditation on the truths of the faith. This process became clear to Waugh when he compared the confused, secretive rituals of the Abyssinian Church with the liturgy of the West. In *Remote People*, he writes:

At Debra Lebanos I suddenly saw the classic basilica and open altar as a great positive achievement, a triumph of light over darkness consciously accomplished, and I saw theology as the science of simplification by which nebulous and elusive ideas are formalised and made intelligible and exact. I saw the Church of the first century as a dark hidden thing . . . the pure nucleus of the truth lay in the minds of the people, encumbered with superstitions, gross survivals of . . . paganism . . . hazy and obscene nonsense seeping in from the other esoteric cults of the Near East, magical infections from the conquered barbarian. And I began to see how these obscure sanctuaries had grown, with the clarity of Western reason, into the great open altars of Catholic Europe, where Mass is said in a flood of light, high in the sight of all. (pp. 88–9)

The exercise of reason leads the mind to an infallible Church; the exercise of that infallibility in turn incites the minds of the faithful to further reasoning, but always within an authoritatively established and essentially conservative system.

Catholicism thus solved for Waugh the problem of disconnection. In particular it restored to him the attachments of patriotism, while confirming his detachment from unthinking devotion to King and Country. The Church, Knox writes,

is . . . the analogue of a nation or country . . . In this sublime creation of Providence, all that has given birth to the clan, the tribe, the nation, the club, is pressed into a higher service and acquires a supernatural character. The Church is our Mother, in that her baptism gives us supernatural life; our

Mistress, in that her teaching secures us from speculative error; but she is more than that; she is ourselves. (p. 191)

Waugh's new homeland was Christian Europe, and the remnants of Catholic life which survived in Britain (see Stannard, pp. 219–23). He acknowledged the fascination of paganism, but resisted its blandishments as, in their different ways, Kipling and Forster had failed to do. At the same time he acknowledged his own and everyone else's sinfulness and thereby re-established unembarrassed contact with his non-believing friends; he viewed lax sexual behaviour differently now, but he did not claim to be unfamiliar with it. He was not graced with heroic sanctity; he was just a practising Catholic, who knew the rules, obeyed them for the most part, and sought absolution without excuses and with real contrition when he did not. Above all he could believe in reason, but as the servant, not the source of certitude. The socio-historical connections in human affairs for which Father Rothschild had feebly sought were therefore irrelevant. The pessimism of *Vile Bodies* had been the result of a desire for the wrong kind of answer.

We have still to account, however, for Waugh's next book, *Black Mischief*. In the words of Ernest Oldmeadow, editor of the Catholic weekly, the *Tablet*, its 'coarseness and foulness' (*Letters*, p. 72) cast doubt on Waugh's Catholic credentials. 'The novel . . .', Oldmeadow wrote,

is about an imaginary island in the Indian Ocean, ruled by a black Emperor. Prudence, daughter of the British Minister at the Emperor's court, goes up to the unsavoury room (the soapy water unemptied) of Basil, a man she hardly knows, and, after saying, 'You might have shaved' and 'Please help with my boots,' stays till there is 'a banging on the door.' In the end, Basil, at a cannibal feast, unwittingly helps to eat the body of Prudence 'stewed to pulp amid peppers and aromatic roots.' In working out this foul invention, Mr. Waugh gives us disgusting passages. We are introduced to a young couple dining in bed, with 'a bull terrier and a chow flirting on their feet.' The young wife suddenly calls out 'Oh God, he's made a mess again'; and Basil exclaims 'How dirty the bed is.' These nasty details are not necessary to the story. A dozen silly pages are devoted to a Birth Control Pageant, announced by posters which flaunt all over the island 'a detailed drawing of some up-to-date contraceptive apparatus.' The Emperor 're-names the site of the Anglican Cathedral "Place Marie Stopes." ' Two humane ladies are ridiculed; in one place so indelicately that the passage cannot be described by us. There is a comic description of a Nestorian monastery with a venerated cross 'which had fallen from heaven quite unexpectedly during Good Friday luncheon, some years back.' If the twelve signatories of the above protest find nothing wrong with 'during Good Friday luncheon' we cannot help them. (*Letters*, p. 73)

The twelve signatories had written to Oldmeadow protesting at an earlier attack on Waugh. They included four priests, and several distinguished writers and artists; evidently the novel did not offend everyone of Catholic sensibility and conviction. Moreover, reading Oldmeadow's diatribe today (notably his objection to the behaviour of the dogs), one can see that what really upset him was the violation of taboos governing the printed word. Nevertheless there is substance to his complaints. The details of the scene in Sonia and Alastair's bedroom *are* nasty. It is a relief to discover that the likeable Alastair has found himself a nice wife, but the slump has reduced their honest hedonism to mean dimensions. Equally, what is disturbing in Prudence's seduction is that the hitherto ridiculous Prudence is suddenly vulnerable, and the urbane Basil unexpectedly diminished by a sad sordid setting which surprisingly anticipates the Africa of Graham Greene – 'In the bath water, the soggy stub of tobacco emanated a brown blot of juice' (p. 130). But it is not the characters or the setting so much as the ambivalent responses elicited from the reader that are potentially compromising to Catholic values. The same applies to the treatment of the 'humane ladies'. Waugh claimed that this charge failed on two grounds – that they were not humane and that they were not real but fictional characters. This is disingenuous. His treatment of Dame Mildred and Miss Trim incites the reader to take a sadistic relish in their humiliations. Finally there is the problem of blasphemy. Again, Oldmeadow has a point. It is precisely the inappropriately urbane 'luncheon', rather than the phoniness of the miracle, which is insulting to religious sensibility. But Oldmeadow missed the ultimate blasphemy in the novel: the eating of Prudence is dangerously like a parody of the Eucharist. However he did pick up the implications of Waugh's treatment of this incident. In focusing on the peppers and aromatic roots, the narrative devalues Prudence and everything she *might* signify.

Another problem which Oldmeadow failed to examine was that of race. In the Port Said brothel four native girls are gratuitously described as huddling together 'in the corner like chimpanzees' (p. 84). Later, the outrageously named Black Bitch lifts 'her dress . . . and [wipes] her hands on her knickers' (p. 123) before accepting a dinner invitation to the French Legation. We are even asked to believe that the Azanians think Dame Mildred and Miss Trim are in favour of cruelty to animals, while Seth's only comment on the Wanda's killing Seyid and eating him is that they are 'barbarous . . . totally out of touch with modern thought. They need education . . . We might start them on Montessori methods' (pp. 40–1).

Black Mischief thus clearly threatens values of many kinds, including those of Christianity and principled anti-racialism. It does so above all because it is well written. Like *Decline and Fall*, it can be read with pleasure at the level of form, but this encourages the reader to condone its reckless treatment of the human element at the level of life. The question we need to address, therefore, is whether the experience of switching one's attention between these levels discloses (as it does in *Decline and Fall*) a stance which acknowledges the value-systems of each but is identical with neither. And to answer that question we need to read *Black Mischief* as an arrangement of Waugh's thoughts for his existing audience – the public that bought his books in large numbers on the one hand, and his intimate, inscribed readership on the other.

We can begin with the latter. As usual, Waugh playfully maps his own private world on to that of the novel. Cruttwell is a 'very silly' last-minute guest at Lady Seal's dinner party (p. 78). General Connolly is named after the urbane Cyril Connolly. As the latter's wife at that time was dark complexioned, the General's marriage to Black Bitch is presumably another joke. Basil Seal is partly based on Nancy Mitford's first husband, and the corrupt and cowardly Viscount Boaz is given the nickname Waugh used of himself in his letters to the Lygon sisters and Lady Diana Cooper. A different kind of mapping establishes a more public network of relationships between the novel and its contexts. For example, by giving an officer of the imperial guard the name Joab, Waugh establishes parallels between his story and The Second Book of Samuel. Joab arranges the murders of Ali in Chapter One and Boaz in Chapter Seven. His brutal and cunning biblical namesake similarly arranges the death of David's son, Absalom, when the latter's rebellion fails. An example of Waugh's immaculate timing occurs at the end of Chapter One when Seth casually mentions that Seyid was his father, thus reversing the biblical story which concludes with David's celebrated lament for Absalom. In some ways, Seth is David's feeble antithesis, but other parallels are more confusing, particularly the reminder that politics are as squalid in sacred as in profane history.

Funnier and no less significant is the mapping of British and European experience on to Azanian life. Initially the Azanians' titles seem uncomfortably like a cheap colonialist joke, but they are just one aspect of a game with inappropriate language in the novel which makes Europe look as foolish as Africa. Waugh projects some serious satire of European Catholicism, for example, on to the Nestorian Church. It was not in Africa but in France that 'muscular Christians' were eager 'to have a whack at the modernists and Jews' (p. 177). The British and French Legations are equally diminished by verbal caricature. The British talk of gardening, games and schools, the French of conspiracy and militant secularism. Each is as racially stereotyped, as silly as the Azanians' appropriation of Western vocabulary. Similarly it is by mixing incompatible vocabularies that the Earl of Ngumo is perceived as archetypal cannibal chief and Highland laird.

These linguistic games make Waugh's treatment of race very different from Kipling's. 'Without Benefit of Clergy' in *Life's Handicap*, presents the tragic love story of a young colonial official and a Muslim girl whom he has literally bought from her impoverished mother; the girl bears him a beautiful male child, whose unexpected death is quickly followed by that of his mother. Kipling opens his story with a stylized dialogue in which neither lover is named and which is suggestive of Urdu. The reader is thereby led into thinking that the lovers are both Indians, and has then to adjust to the disclosure that this inter-racial, extra-marital and mercenary relationship is also authentically human. Waugh's presentation of Connolly and Black Bitch is linguistically much more superficial; our curiosity about it is constantly deflected by the sense that each is a construct, a joke. But the conclusion of their story is more serious than that of Holden and Ameera's. Connolly is a simple characterization but a complex figure. He is a stereotype of the honest soldier, yet he has a sinister background. Though the bearer of an Irish name, he has served in the Black and Tans as well as the South African Police and the Kenya Game Reserves. First he defeats Seth's enemies; then he conspires against Seth, after a petty quarrel with Basil. Finally, he is illegally expelled from Azania by the protecting powers, mainly because of his happy marriage to a black woman. Thus though less rounded than Kipling's Holden, he is more difficult to interpret. The issues Kipling raises are psychological and moral, but the meanings attaching to Connolly are political. He is the product, the agent and the victim of imperialism, a focus for its innumerable deceptions and self-deceptions. The ambivalence of our reactions to him entrap us in historical contradictions which Kipling conveniently resolves in the deaths of the mother and her child.

But the real challenge of *Black Mischief* emerges in Waugh's treatment of Seth and Basil. Alone of the Azanians, Seth is accorded full human status. He is a type both of the individual of intelligence and good will on which Forsterian liberalism is based and of the *déraciné* victim of imperialism. (In neither respect is he at all like the adroit Ras Tafari.) Seth takes what comfort he can from his imperial proclamations and liberal slogans – 'I have seen the great tattoo at Aldershot, the Paris Exhibition, the Oxford Union . . . at my stirrups run woman's suffrage, vaccination and vivisection' (p. 16). Not surprisingly, his notions of civilization are drawn from advertisers' catalogues. Like all the other characters except Basil, his experience and significance are indicated by means of grotesque collisions of inappropriate idiom, but the results in his case, though funny, are never reductive. We are always aware of his pain and his proximity to disaster:

Seth lay awake and alone, his eyes wild with the inherited terror of the jungle, desperate with the acquired loneliness of civilization. Night was alive with beasts and devils and the spirits of dead enemies; before its power Seth's ancestors had receded . . . abandoning in retreat all the baggage of Individuality; they had lain six or seven in a hut; between them and night only a wall of mud and a ceiling of thatched grass; warm, naked bodies . . . invisibly unified so that they ceased to be six or seven scared blacks and became one person of more than human stature . . . Seth . . . was alone, dwarfed by the magnitude of the darkness, insulated from his fellows, strapped down to mean dimensions. (p. 25)

If this is what civilization does to Seth, we may surely conclude that barbaric terrors and barbaric communion would be better – for Africa as well as for himself.

The other loner in the novel, the antithesis of Seth and of Forsterian man, is Basil. The impression he makes is greatly assisted by his partner in uncompromising selfishness, Mr Youkoumian. Our licensed laughter at Mrs Youkoumian's expense and her husband's devotion to the main chance and his own comfort effects a moral clearing of the decks which ensure that we take seriously the less innocent comedy of Basil's conduct. He seduces us as he seduces Prudence. We condone his theft of his mother's emerald bracelet because that is the just reward of her incapacity, and Sir Joseph's, to admit the truth about him, but we find ourselves in the same situation as they were in when he subsequently exploits both Prudence and Seth for his own whimsical purposes. It is our own moral embarrassment which makes Basil's subsequent loyalty to Seth so important. But Basil then eats Prudence and, to our great disquiet, returns unruffled to his old life.

Of course Basil is only the prompter of such feelings. It is the book as a whole that has trapped us. We have accepted flippant allusions to cannibalism, public executions, nudity and slavery. An additional frisson to the comedy has been our awareness of atrocity, that contraceptive-users in Azania may be dismembered by a laughing Earl of Ngumo. The comic tone remained intact even when we confronted the shambling son of the great Amurath, kept chained and naked in a cave for decades by astute Nestorian monks. But in the end, the condescending, half-considered sense we may have entertained that Seth and Africa would be better off in the intimate communion of the jungle is shattered by what such communion involves. Cannibal 'wise men', wearing 'leopards' feet and snake skins, amulets and necklaces, lions' teeth and the shrivelled bodies of bats and toads, jigging and spinning' (p. 214) against a background of tireless drumming and 'glistening backs heaving and shivering in the shadows' are a far cry from Kipling's proto-fascist view of the jungle as a chaste paradigm of dignity, courage and wisdom. Here, in a sense which I shall explore more closely in my discussion of *The Loved One* (1948), is Evil.

An equally important difference between Waugh and Kipling is his adoption of a narratorial stance which blocks all explanation or exculpation. In this respect his exact counterpart in the text is Basil, who is 'so *teaching*' (p. 66) about Indian dialects he cannot speak and about the world's monetary systems, but who is taciturn to a degree about himself. According to the ancient formula, Christians at their baptism renounce the world, the flesh and the devil. But in Catholic teaching, the world, though fallen, is not utterly corrupt. It remains an arena in which it is possible to practice the natural 'Aristotelian' virtues. Basil accordingly has three important qualities we may properly admire – self-assurance, clear-sightedness and fortitude. His London friends have self-assurance, but they cultivate a sophisticated myopia which leaves their fortitude untested. Mr Youkoumian is clear-sighted but he is a coward. Connolly is self-assured and courageous but lacks self-awareness. The rest are insecure, confused and cowardly at the same time, and they use language to conceal the fact. Wherever it occurs – in the speeches of Seth, or M. Ballon, or Sir Samson Courteney, or Prudence, or Sir Joseph Mainwaring – fluency of utterance seeks vainly to suggest that the speaker is at home in the world, and that the speaker's values – progress, reason, comfort, romance or appearances – are secure as well. Even the dignified Arab gentlemen of Matodi maintain their place in the scheme of things by words. Only Basil's virtues are silent.

Except, of course, that Waugh's are also. In certain respects he puts himself on record – his fascination with barbaric nakedness and elegant urbanity; his appreciation of cynicism and unabashed selfishness; his love of order, verbal elegance and structural deftness; his affection for naïvety; his cold-heartedness; his exacting notions of conduct; his capacity for cruel glee. But he is not prepared to explain. Basil's relations with the other characters, and particularly with his friends in London after his return from Azania, thus echo Waugh's relations with his readers. Basil refuses to tell Alastair and Sonia that their frivolous guesses about his adventures are deadly accurate, and Waugh refuses to disclose how his known beliefs relate to the radically atheistical worldliness of his central character. 'Behold the man of the world', says the Catholic novelist, and then refuses to say whether he himself is to be counted as another such or not.

We are left, then, with this question: is Waugh's reserve the same kind of thing as Basil's? Basil's principal virtue is fortitude. Self-assurance is a condition of this fortitude, and clear-sightedness a measure of its scope. He survives, however, only by ruthlessly restricting the attention he gives to other people. His relationship with Angela Lyne is founded on her acceptance of this solipsism: he talks obsessively about what interests him, and that includes Angela's money, but never about his feelings or hers. He avoids the contradictions which the others hide from with self-deluding explanation by pursuing a policy of avoidance in personal relationships. This suggests that Basil's world is an arena of limited order and essential disconnection, from which meaning is absent and in which only the clever, privileged egotist can expect to flourish. This cannot be Waugh's position. Firstly, there is the obvious, logical consideration that in signifying Basil's limitations, particularly in his behaviour towards Prudence, Waugh's point of view is necessarily distinct from (if not necessarily superior to) that of his creation. More significant, however, is the comprehensiveness of Waugh's reserve. Unlike Conrad or Kipling or Forster, he does not infuse his storytelling with a note of personal authority, with wisdom, kindliness, scepticism or compassion. His tone is as casual as the studied nonchalance of Basil's replies to Alastair and Sonia in the last chapter. He thereby avoids association even with the fortitude which is Basil's virtue in chief. His perspectives are thus carefully distinguished from Basil's, but they are not disclosed.

Waugh's position in *Black Mischief*, I suggest, is analogous to the principle of reserve espoused by Cardinal Newman. Some religious truths, Newman taught, and particularly such difficult yet fundamental doctrines as the Atonement, could not be offered wholesale to the unbeliever because unbelief was inconsistent with sensitive apprehension of the doctrine; apologetics was the art of controlled disclosure (Roderick Strange, *Newman and the Gospel of Christ*, 1981, pp. 102–5). Waugh's manner of asserting, and keeping quiet about, his most deeply held beliefs, at least in the novels of the 1930s, seems to operate along similar lines. Catholicism is a sign in *Black Mischief* by virtue of its quite provocative absence. (The brief references to the Canadian missionary function merely as reminders of that absence.) The reader desperately wants to know where the author stands, but has to be taught that certitude of the kind which permits unflinching clear-sightedness about the world and frankness about oneself, certitude, in short, which can look Basil in the eye, is finally a private matter.

Writing *Vile Bodies*, Waugh had found himself isolated in a no man's land between pious and honourable decencies, in which he had been unable to believe since adolescence, and a resolutely sophisticated jungle of fashionable hedonism, from which he was suddenly and devastatingly estranged. By 1939, he was able to endorse the 'positive work' of the conservative, to approve the achievements of pious and honourable people, while claiming for himself the privileges of 'a dissident'. In *Robbery Under Law*, as we have seen, he argues that it is the task of 'a dissident' to remind the world that 'we are all potential recruits for anarchy', and to invite the public to a sort of notional orgy. This is an 'agreeable' position: it has 'all the solid advantages of other people's creation and preservation, and all the fun of detecting hypocrisies and inconsistencies. There are times,' Waugh suggests, 'when dissidents are not only enviable but valuable' (p. 279). It is not the dissident's task, in other words, to obey the Forsterian injunction to connect, but rather to cross the frontiers, mental or geographical, between imperial connectedness and barbaric anarchy and, while relying on the forces of law and order to keep things going, to indulge the appetites of chaos as he chooses.

This, paradoxically, applies especially to the Catholic dissident, the confessor and martyr, like Campion, the writer like Waugh. Both enjoy the privileges of reserve. The martyr goes on public record, but as an icon of faithfulness, not as an explanation. The Catholic writer (in the infinitely humbler and possibly unedifying role of dissident) has a different but related significance. Detecting hypocrisies and inconsistencies puts civil society and therefore the agreeable position of the non-Catholic dissident in real jeopardy, but the Catholic has a rock of divine authority and the shared certitudes of the Faithful to fall back on. It is precisely as a Catholic, therefore, that Waugh finds himself curiously but tellingly in harmony with *both* Basil Seal the solipsist and Edmund Campion the Martyr. In their respective fashions, each has silently got the measure of the world.

For more than a decade after his conversion Waugh refused to use his novels as vehicles for his beliefs. Only by maintaining an unqualified silence in the face of the disconnection which they identified could he *enact* the strength of his own certitude. Perhaps the writer who comes closest to him in this respect is Swift, another conservative Christian in thrall to the daemonic, whose eye for inconsistency and disconnection was also matched by a resolution not to supply his readers with explanations. It might possibly have reassured Oldmeadow, therefore, if he had been able to see twentieth-century Catholicism standing beside *Black Mischief* as eighteenth-century Anglicanism had once stood beside the Fourth Part of *Gulliver's Travels*, astonished and mute but not betrayed.

Formally and thematically, Waugh's next novel, *A Handful of Dust* (1934) is virtually a negative version of its predecessor. Once again Waugh's new faith is represented only to emphasize its absence: in *Black Mischief* the only Catholic character is the Canadian White Father, in *A Handful of Dust* the young girl, Thérèse de Vitré, with whom Tony Last has his failed ship-board romance. (This episode is said to be a reflection of Waugh's hopeless entanglement with 'Baby' Jungman.) Like its predecessor, *A Handful of Dust* mixes the world of the English upper class with that of a primitive people, but in proportions that reverse those of the earlier novel. The key point of correspondence and contrast, however, is between Basil and Tony. Tony is like Basil in two respects; he is the only character to move between the novel's two worlds, and he has important natural virtues. But Tony's virtues – decency, courtesy, loyalty and honour – are the opposite of Basil's, and while Basil strictly upholds his version of the principle of reserve, Tony is committed to explanation and so is prey to forces outside himself which Basil has under control. Basil would never have dished his chances with Thérèse by blurting out the facts of his past life. But each provokes the same question. What kind of a world is it that allows a man like Tony to fail, or one like Basil to succeed? The answer in each case (implied though never stated) is a world comprehensively in need of redemption.

This 'world' was no abstraction for Waugh. Travel and his conversion gave him, as we have seen, a strong sense of the importance of history. Accordingly, in establishing his fictional island of Azania (a transposition of Abyssinia on to Zanzibar), he made its history consistent with the recent African past. The situation in *A Handful of Dust* is more complicated. The history of England haunts the text, but only because its characters rely on that inadequate 'sense of period' over which Waugh himself had puzzled in *Labels*:

a vague knowledge of History, Literature, and Art, an amateurish interest in architecture and costume, of social, religious, and political institutions, of drama, of the biographies of the chief characters of each century, of a few memorable anecdotes and jokes, scraps of diaries and correspondence and family history. (p. 48)

This amorphous sense of the past leads to its reconstitution as myth, an effect which Kipling *wanted* to achieve, and which Forster was compelled to resort to at the end of *A Passage to India*, but which Waugh despises. In *A Handful of Dust* and in later works, notably *Helena* (1950), myths function as false consciousness for Waugh, as self-deceiving forms of consolation and explanation. Myths of 'England', of Class, and of Family, for example, sustain the inadequate notions of piety and honour which inform Tony's life, though because he is the owner of Hetton, his reconstruction of the

past is less confused than Mrs Hoop's in *Vile Bodies*. But it is quite
as unreal. This is itself part of history. Hetton, after all, is an
example of bad Victorian Gothic, a monument to the inadequacy of
an earlier generation's sense of period. Tony's notion of how his
ancestors conducted themselves simply repeats in a later mode the
sentimental evocations of the past in Victorian architecture, painting and literature. The entire structure of pious and honourable
gentility in English life is thus founded across the generations on a
radically inadequate historical sense which is still in place at the end
of the novel, since Tony himself becomes a mythical figure when the
Richard Lasts succeed him and attempt, probably in vain, to keep
Hetton going. In this respect English society is as mapless as that of
the Amazon: in both worlds the present defines itself by constituting
a past which is merely an arbitrary assemblage of signs, as randomly
dislocated as Revd Tendril's sermons and as incapable of yielding
certitude or stability.

This ridiculing of myth in the novel gives a peculiar twist to its
relation with *The Waste Land* from which it takes its title. Both
works deal in fragments and broken images, the themes of the Quest
and the City, the legends of King Arthur, the lack of meaning and
direction in the contemporary world, the sterility of modern sexual
experience, and the impoverishment of modern English. But the
poem signifies this aridity by pointing to the decay of myth and myth
is precisely what Waugh, as a Catholic, has come to distrust.
Consequently where Madame Sosostris's misuse of the Tarot pack
in *The Waste Land* is apparently symptomatic of a deep-seated
cultural malaise, the incident in the novel which alludes to that
episode – Mrs Northcote telling fortunes by reading the soles of her
clients' feet – is simply a joke. It is not the devaluation of symbol
which concerns Waugh, but the helplessness and humiliation of his
characters. None of Eliot's dazed and demoralized personages, for
example, would be capable of the acute sense of shame which grips
Brenda when she realizes what she has said on learning that it is not
her lover but her son who has been killed. *A Handful of Dust* does
not simply transpose Eliot's vision into another mode. On the
contrary, many of its more striking meanings derive from its being
positively unlike the poem.

Among the most important of these differences is Waugh's awareness of human decency – Ben Hacket's relation with John Andrew, the excellent behaviour (very 'English', controlled and courteous) of everybody at the inquest, and perhaps most surprisingly of all the engaging simplicity of the characters Tony meets in Brighton. The text plays quietly and subtly with incipient racialism – the resolute little Jenny Abdul Akbar has an unsettling conversation with John Andrew (p. 87) about Ben's robust assertions concerning animals, Blacks and Jews. This prepares the ground for Baby's nasty remark in the Brighton hotel, 'This place stinks of yids' (p. 138), to which Tony replies, 'I always think that's the sign of a good hotel, don't you?'. Tony may be making a moral point here or he may merely be exemplifying Newman's honourable but limited 'definition of a gentleman . . . [as] one who never inflicts pain'. A further complication is that Dan, Baby's companion, may himself be Jewish – he is vulgarly flash with his money and his clothes which suggests Waugh may be deliberately evoking another racial stereotype. But Dan's friend takes good care of Tony at the party, and Tony wonders 'whether he was as amiable when people he did not know were brought over unexpectedly to Hetton' (p. 140). This sudden intrusion of the human element, in the context of some decidedly cruel and superficially snobbish farce, comes as a relief. It is not the kind of experience one gets from *The Waste Land* and confirms one's sense that the worlds of the poem and the novel are different, and that the diagnosis of the novelist is not that of the poet.

At the heart of this difference is Tony's innocence and natural goodness. This gives the characterization of Brenda its subtlety and seriousness, for it is his trust of her that makes her behaviour towards him so wicked and her shame so acute. This was important to Waugh since the story of Brenda's defection bore closely on his own experience. Putting it on record, however indirectly, was a further instance of his willingness to outface his public, to maintain his poise, while keeping in reserve the point of view which enabled him to do so. It was essential, therefore, that his treatment of Brenda should be just. Accordingly (to use a distinction developed by Catholic philosophers), he presents her as corrupt in her will, not like Marjorie, Allan, Polly and Jenny, who are corrupt in their understanding. In closing ranks behind her, her family and friends are simply thoughtless and callous after the fashion of their kind, but, having lived with Tony and manipulated him, Brenda has an appalled self-knowingness which they cannot share. In this she is a feminine version of Adam Fenwyck-Symes. Interestingly, in each case, money not sex motivates their really wicked behaviour: anyone can fall victim to sexual obsession, but selling your fiancée, or bleeding your husband of his patrimony to satisfy a parasitic lover, constitutes serious wrong-doing. Yet Brenda never becomes a merely despicable figure. When Tony goes abroad, she is temporally demoralized and impoverished, but her real punishment has been to see her situation accurately from the beginning. She thus retains her capacity for self-directed irony: 'I was never one for making myself expensive,' she says (p. 191) when Beaver lets her see herself home. Wit of this kind is a sign of grace in Waugh, though not of the grace that sanctifies. She only surrenders her essential identity in the brilliant intercutting between London and the jungle when she is symbolically reunited with Tony and both are reduced to the tears and anger of the nursery. In all his later writings (with one exception in *Brideshead Revisited* [1945]), Waugh maintained a stance of uncensorious, unsentimental compassion towards faithless women.

The treatment of Tony is more problematical. The novel began as a short story, which was published in the United States as 'The Man Who Liked Dickens' and told the story of Tony's imprisonment by Mr Todd; 'eventually the thing grew into a study of other sorts of savage at home and the civilized man's hopeless plight among them' (*Essays*, p. 303). For copyright reasons an American serialization of the novel has a different ending: Tony returns to London, rescues Brenda from poverty, and takes over the London flat to prosecute his own adulteries. This is a much more comfortable conclusion than the one we are given. Henry Yorke found the English ending 'so fantastic that it throws the rest out of proportion . . . The first part,' he told Waugh, was 'convincing, a real picture of people one has met and may at any moment meet again' (*Letters*, p. 88), but the Mr Todd sequence was 'fantasy' because 'natives' were *never* honest. In other words 'natives' were *both* unreal *and* unable to behave as 'we' do. The contradiction exposes why Yorke found the canonical ending unsatisfactory. He wanted to circumscribe the 'real', to keep it within 'the Pale'. But Waugh knew better: he had met people like the Macushi and the Pie-wie in British Guiana; he had even met the original of Mr Todd (*Diaries*, pp. 366–7): 'the Amazon stuff,' he insisted, 'had to be there. The scheme was a Gothic man in the hands of savages – first Mrs Beaver, etc. then the real ones, finally the silver foxes at Hetton' (*Letters*, p. 88). Barbarism is never defeated. We are all potential recruits for the Pie-wie. In the end it is Yorke's conception of what 'a real picture' can include, and his confidence about how 'natives' differ from 'people one has met', which are limited and fantastic.

The problem with the Todd episode is not that it is fantastic, but that it is arbitrary. As a *tour de force* of filmic cross-cutting, the Amazonian scenes are evidently the wilful construction of an artist-craftsman, and are therefore in violation of norms set up in the English section which operates in the manner of classical comedy as a single action arising naturally out of clearly delineated circumstances and clearly motivated characters. Had it kept to these norms, the novel would have become an analogue of a game of Patience played to a successful conclusion, unlike the game played by Mrs Rattery while she and Tony sit it out at Hetton in the dreadful hours after John Andrew's death. Mrs Rattery is a striking conception, a female Basil Seal who is always in command of herself, and at the same time a symbolic, almost portentous figure:

(Mrs Rattery sat intent over her game, moving little groups of cards adroitly backward and forwards about the table like shuttles across a loom; under her fingers order grew out of chaos; she established sequence and precedence; the symbols before her became coherent, interrelated.) . . .
Mrs Rattery brooded over her chequer of cards and then drew them towards her into a heap, haphazard once more and without meaning; it had nearly come to a solution that time, but for a six of diamonds out of place, and a stubbornly congested patch at one corner, where nothing could be made to move. 'It's a heart-breaking game,' she said. (pp. 110–1)

What Yorke really wanted, one suspects, was for the action of the novel to 'come to a solution' within a 'civilized' frame of reference. The American serial, with its 'happy ending', does just this, but only by endorsing the relativistic view of meaning and personality which Mrs Rattery's game symbolizes. By transforming Tony into a cynical adulterer, the American version reinstates the world-view of Marjorie and Allan, for whom a person's identity is entirely generated by the rules currently in play, whether they are those of the West End or chez Todd.

But the novel as published refuses to come to a solution in this way. It also avoids the other route to an ending taken by Conrad's *Heart of Darkness*, on which its closing section is apparently modelled. Admittedly Tony fails to find his City, he fails to discover a meaning, but the heartless bravura with which Waugh narrates this failure prohibits our concluding that, like a latter-day Marlowe, Tony has discovered meaninglessness on our behalf. The consciousness that commands our attention at this stage is the author's not his protagonist's, and the question demanding an answer relates to the unconcealed high spirits of the narration. The tension generated between formal wit and human suffering in the last three chapters of *A Handful of Dust* is more acute than anything in the earlier novels. The simultaneous excitements of the pig hunt on the Amazon and Jock Grant-Menzies' questions in the House, so carefully anticipated in earlier chapters; the audacity of having a flagrantly Dickensian character like Mr Todd demanding to be feasted on Dickens to the end of his days; the economy with which all the narrative lines are concluded in the closing pages – all this generates admiration as it resists explanation.

Nor is an explanation ever supplied. Instead we are given a sign, in the person of Thérèse de Vitré. Perhaps because of its autobiographical source, Waugh told Yorke that he thought 'the sentimental episode with Thérèse in the ship [was] probably a mistake' (*Letters*, p. 88). He need not have worried. This allegedly sentimental episode is remarkably tough. Thérèse enjoys no natural protection from forces outside herself. Her innocence is ignorance, her lack of worldliness naïvety, her future happiness in an arranged marriage far from assured. Her father – 'the complete slave-owner of the last century' (p. 167) – is a sharp reminder that the political record of Catholic civilization is not invariably superior to that of its Protestant counterpart. Yet her essential identity is not at risk. She alone carries the secret of certitude in the book, the knowledge that natural virtues, such as Tony's (and indeed her own), can make no claims on Providence, that, in the words of the Epistle to the Hebrews, 'we have not here a permanent city but we seek that which is to come' (13:14, Douai). The effectiveness with which the principle of reserve imposed itself on Waugh in the writing of even this crucial episode may be measured by the fleeting presence of what Thérèse thus signifies in the text as a whole, but it is sufficient, I believe, to account for the paradoxical ebullience with which the novel works out its heartbreaking conclusion.

Waugh's next novel, *Scoop*, appeared in 1938. In the intervening four years he made two visits to Abyssinia, the first as war correspondent for the *Daily Mail* following Mussolini's invasion in 1935, and the second to see how things were after the Italians had won – he had left Abyssinia thinking they were going to be beaten. Waugh was not a satisfactory newspaper man. His pro-Italian views made him unpopular with the other correspondents and the Abyssinian authorities; the British Minister and his family had (not surprisingly) found *Black Mischief* offensive; he missed a major story by being out of Addis Ababa at the wrong time, and he cabled his one big scoop in Latin, which no one at the *Mail* could read. Eventually he was sacked, but stayed on stubbornly until the end of 1935. But for the company of his old friend Patrick Balfour (later Baron Kinross), the *Evening Standard*'s correspondent, his time in Abyssinia would have been intolerable. Like everyone else covering the war, he was kept well away from the front. 'No one is allowed to leave Addis' he wrote to Laura Herbert, 'so all those adventures I came for will not happen. Sad. Still all this will make a funny novel so it isn't wasted' (*Letters*, p. 100).

It wasn't, but the funny novel took some time to write. Shortly after he returned to England, his first marriage was finally anulled; he became engaged to Laura (thirteen years his junior) and married her; Laura's mother bought them a fine house in Gloucestershire; he was paid for preparing film scenarios, none of which was produced; and he wrote the unhappily titled *Waugh in Abyssinia* (1936), as well as numerous newspaper articles. *Campion* had been a great success and was awarded the Hawthornden Prize. He was now committed to domesticity after years of nomadic promiscuity. He was happy, and this is one reason why his funny novel is different from its predecessors.

The word Waugh was to use of it is 'light' (Stannard, pp. 471, 472). The formal and human elements are not in tension; the characters do not struggle to maintain their essential identity; the newspaper world is coarse and foolish, its dimensions grandiose yet morally mean, but its self-absorption threatens no one, and in any case it meets its match in the thick-skinned Boots, each of whom exhibits something of Colonel Blount's myopic cunning but who collectively are a genial and harmless bunch. *Scoop* comes to a solution without anyone's heart being broken; the be-ers win hands down over the becomers except for 'plain Mr Baldwin' who wins hands down over everybody. Yet it is a highly characteristic performance. Once again Waugh offers portraits of his friends to the knowing reader, notably Mrs Julia Stitch (an affectionate study of Lady Diana Cooper), William Boot (the young William Deedes – now Sir William – whom Waugh befriended in Abyssinia), Lord Copper (Lord Beaverbrook, founder of Express Newspapers), and at least two journalists, Sir Jocelyn Hitchcock (Sir Percival Philips) and Wenlock Jakes (the American, H. R. Knickerbocker), both recalled from Waugh's days in Addis. Like the earlier novels, *Scoop* is carefully crafted. Reviewing Cyril Connolly's *Enemies of Promise* in 1938, Waugh argued that a writer needs the

energy and breadth of vision to conceive and complete a structure . . . writing is an art which exists in a time sequence; each page is dependent on its predecessors and successors; a sentence . . . may owe its significance to another fifty pages distant. (*Essays*, p. 239)

He systematically revised *Scoop* to achieve such effects, developing the figures of Baldwin, Benito and Corker, and the theme of lush places in this fashion (Stannard, p. 474).

There are also broader affinities with its predecessors. *Scoop* might almost be subtitled, 'Variations on some themes by the same composer' – one of its abiding pleasures being Waugh's expert recycling of old material as well as his development of new ideas for subsequent use. (The Boot household, as well as parodying the settings of P. G. Wodehouse and Ivy Compton-Burnett, reads like an anticipatory parody of Brideshead.) William Boot is Paul Penny-feather in the world of Basil Seal. His story is a fantasy-nightmare from which the young protagonist returns safely to his original condition, but Waugh varies this second telling in the interest of lightness. Both protagonists are used and abandoned by the women who sexually initiate them, but Kätchen is a less unsettling seduc-tress than Margot. Each finally gets off the Wheel, but whereas William removes himself from the clutches of the *Beast* with an upper-class hauteur Paul could never quite have carried off, Paul acquires an avuncular maturity William will never need:

> 'I've felt an ass for weeks. Ever since I went to London. I've been treated like an ass . . . It's one thing being an ass in Africa. But if I go to this banquet they may learn about it down here . . . Nanny Bloggs and Nanny Price and everyone.' (p. 210)

The childish language suggests that William's defences are as secure as those of Captain Grimes. There are affinities also between *Scoop* and *A Handful of Dust* and again the effect is a lightening of the tension. Mr Salter becomes a Tony Last figure and rural England his heart of darkness, 'where you never [know] from one minute to the next that you might not be tossed by a bull or pitch-forked by a yokel or rolled over and broken up by a pack of hounds' (p. 27). He meets his Pie-wie Indians in the persons of the sly, incapable lorry driver and the blind Bert Tyler, and his Mr Todd (multiplied and varied) in the occupants of Boot Hall. This rural jungle is an image of both Fleet Street and Ishmaelia, but with none of the troublesome implications which such repetitions and variations have in the earlier novels. On the contrary, the effect of lightness in *Scoop* is largely due to the absence of such anxieties. Like a music hall comic going through some old routines, Waugh springs some happy surprises on an audience who think they know what to expect.

In general, the novel's politics, too, are part of the fun. If *Scoop* playfully draws the frontier between imperial order and barbarian chaos across the southern counties of England, it also mischievously transposes European politics on to Ishmaelia. So the crisis which brings the world's press scurrying to the scene is not an imperialist war, but a competition for mineral rights between the Fascist, Bolshevik and capitalist Powers. Waugh trivializes Right and Left impartially. He invents a Black Fascist movement called the White Shirts and gives Mussolini's Christian name to the leading Bolshevik conspirator. His most elaborate joke is to distribute the names of the heroes of nineteenth- and twentieth-century Liberal, agnostic and progressive causes among the corrupt ruling family of Ishmaelia, the Jacksons. Mrs Earl Russell Jackson puffing her pipe, licking her thumb and turning the pages of the good book is a deeply satisfying conception. But the best joke of all is the impishly successful reworking of Father Rothschild as a multilingual, balletic parachutist and capitalist, of exotic and obscure racial extraction, whose too-beautifully formed sentences belie his repeated and confident claim to be a Britisher, and who assumes for the sake of convenience – and because it is non-committal, British, and above all easily memorable – the surname of the then Prime Minister, Stanley Baldwin.

But there are serious moments even in this most cheerful of books. It contains, as all of Waugh's pre-war novels do, some insolently offensive writing:

'The patriotic cause in Ishmaelia,' he said, 'is the cause of the coloured man and of the proletariat throughout the world. The Ishmaelite worker is threatened by a corrupt and foreign coalition of capitalistic exploiters, priests and imperialists. As that great Negro Karl Marx has so nobly written . . .' He talked for about twenty minutes. The black-backed, pink-palmed, fin-like hands beneath the violet cuffs flapped and slapped . . .
At length he paused and wiped the line of froth from his lips. (p. 50)

This is different from the grotesque description of the blind Bert Tyler and his driving friend, because the object of derision in the later episode is Mr Salter. But such calculated racialism has to be set against the remarkable characterization of the leading Bolshevik in Ishmaelia, Benito, a 'short and brisk and self-possessed' man, 'soot-black in face, with piercing boot-button eyes' (p. 119), who speaks perfect English and French, and has in his face that which even thick-skinned reporters are compelled to call master: – 'As he passed through them the journalists were hushed; it was as though the head-mistress had suddenly appeared among an unruly class of schoolgirls.' Benito is a crafty politician, the one entirely adult human being in the novel, the sort of person one has met and may at any moment meet again – he alone understands how things are connected in Ishmaelia. There is something worrying, therefore, in his being simply bundled off a balcony by a drunken Swede, presumably to his death, leaving the field to the dainty Mr Baldwin. Just once in the entire novel, Waugh allows his joke to turn a little sour.

In the context of Waugh's increasingly alarmed and combative non-fictional writings from 1936 onwards, the remarkable thing about *Scoop* is that this sourness is so restrained. Politically Waugh was becoming increasingly pessimistic. Strongly to the Right, he was also a passionate opponent of Nazism. He even saw the traditional Christmas as loathsome because of its 'Hitlerite adjuncts' (*Letters*, p. 103): Nazism represented the triumph not of the will but of myth, specifically the race myth, a term he used frequently and always with disgust. Unfortunately the principal opponents of German neo-Paganism were Liberals and Marxists who denied the primacy of 'the individual soul (which is the preconception of Christendom)' (*Essays*, p. 204) and the doctrines 'of the Fall of Man and the Atonement' (*Essays*, p. 245) which alone secure us from the delusion 'that only the most flimsy and artificial obstructions keep man from boundless physical well-being'. Waugh's was an anti-market con-servatism: the business of life was not 'buying, selling and manufac-turing and the management of these activities in an equitable way' (*Essays*, p. 230) . . . but 'the stark alternatives of Heaven and Hell' (*Essays*, p. 195). It was the failure of all current political orthodoxies to accept 'the basic assumption . . . that every human being is possessed of free will, reason and personal desires' (quoted in Stannard, p. 462) which led to Waugh's provisional sympathy for Mussolini's regime. By conviction he was 'not a Fascist' and protested against the suggestion that a choice between Marxism and Fascism was imminent (Stannard, p. 452). Initially, indeed, there was even an element of perversity in his support for the Italians in Abyssinia. 'It was fun,' he wrote, 'being pro-Italian when it was an unpopular and (I thought) losing cause' (*Letters*, p. 109). But, as the political situation deteriorated, his ideological isolation ceased to be the source of such trivial satisfactions; the crisis was so acute that the bonds of common understanding and mutual comprehension were being broken.

Scoop thus faces us with a problem rather different from its predecessors. Their silence about important issues constructs a significant authorial silence. But with the important yet minor exception of Benito, the lightness of Waugh's fifth novel signals no such reserve, even though it is more explicitly political than any of his earlier fictions. This is almost certainly a result of Waugh's Abyssinian experience. As a war correspondent he made the alarming discovery that there was no connection between 'news' and history. To Katherine Asquith, a fellow-Catholic and owner of Mells Manor, a centre of upper-class Catholic life and culture, he wrote from Addis Ababa. 'The journalists are lousy competitive hysterical lying' (*Letters*, p. 98). He was particularly disgusted by one sentence in his letter of dismissal from the *Mail*: 'From the beginning it has proved a thoroughly disappointing war to us' (Stannard, p. 414). His contempt for such journalistic attitudes explains the glee with which he treats the absurdity of 'cablese' in *Scoop*. Language in the hands of newspapermen becomes a ludicrous and ignoble barrier between history and the people it is happening to. In the letter to Laura anticipating his funny novel, he also wrote, 'The only trouble is there is no chance of making a serious war book as I hoped' (*Letters*, p. 100). It was not just the remoteness of the fighting that blocked this ambition. Abyssinia brought home to him the difficulty in the modern world of writing about history at all. There was in effect a collective indifference to the honest and accurate use of language. (Waugh probably felt this even more keenly than Orwell.) Thus one reason for the lightness of *Scoop* may be that no other way of writing fiction was available to him after 1935. His journalism, letters and travel books could proclaim a brand of Catholicism which found the opposed faces of history and myth equally repellant, but as a novelist his only resource was farce. The serious war book would have to wait events which would not dissappoint even the *Daily Mail*.

CHAPTER THREE

Arcadians:
Work Suspended, *Put Out More Flags* and *Brideshead Revisited*

When war was declared on 3 September 1939, Waugh was living the life of a wealthy countryman and writer. Laura was pregnant with their second child and he was kept busy gardening and writing articles and the occasional short story. He was also working on a new novel, which he never finished. The surviving fragment is one of the most striking of his fictions, a radical departure from his earlier manner, technically original and psychologically exploratory. He published it under the title *Work Suspended* in two forms. In the first limited edition of 1942, the action takes place in 1932 and is confined to the personal and artistic dilemmas of its hero and narrator, John Plant. The 1949 edition brings the action forward to 1939, and work is suspended on two of Plant's narratives – the detective fiction which he is writing when his father dies, and the autobiographical narrative of what happened to him thereafter. The cause of this second interruption is the outbreak of war.

In addition to Plant's two lost narratives, a third work is also, of course, suspended – the novel which Waugh was writing in the autumn of 1939, in which Plant the writer is made unwittingly to betray Plant the man. This betrayal is clearly implied in the account of Plant's return to his dead father's house, where he is unexpectedly overtaken by sorrow, and realizes that 'the civilized man' (p. 131) is betrayed by language. Up to now, Plant has used language to control strong feeling and maintain his privacy. Even after his moment of weakness he continues to do so, especially in his dealings with the ghastly Atwater and the impassioned Julia. But in that one moment he puts his suffering into words; his emotions assume 'the livery of the defence' and 'pass through the lines . . . that', he declares, 'is how the civilized man is undone'.

In setting up this vulnerable first-person narrator, Waugh was both addressing and disguising his own situation. Plant's defensiveness is a soulless version of the reserve which had hitherto been fundamental to Waugh's own work. Plant's chosen form, the detective story, is like a Waugh novel, a finely crafted construct eschewing personal disclosure, but it takes none of the risks which Waugh took in representing savagery and sexual betrayal. Plant lies unnecessarily in the brothel in Fez, and feels uncomfortable when the consul discovers his patronage of the place. Waugh, too, was a stickler for privacy, but he also wrote comic letters to Lady Mary Lygon about his visits to that very brothel in 1934 (*Letters*, pp. 82, 84). Plant has a distant relationship with his father as Waugh did, but Waugh's father was neither misanthropic nor a forger. Plant is homeless as Waugh had been, but goes house-hunting for motives very different from Waugh's before his marriage. Finally Plant becomes attached to the pregnant wife of a friend as Waugh had to Diana Guinness; but Plant lives in 'fear of making [himself] a sitting shot to the world' (p. 135); in the exchange and mart system which he and his friends operate with women, he keeps emotion separate from desire, and even in his friendships there is 'little love and no trust at all' (p. 171). It was not so with the friend of Alastair Graham, the wooer of 'Baby' Jungman, the husband of Laura Herbert.

The complex acts of self-disclosure and self-protection by the real and purported authors of *Work Suspended* were, of course, destined never to come to a solution but certain strong tendencies in the text emerge clearly enough. One of the most important relates to the problem of form and the human element, a theme apparently represented in the contrast between Roger Simmonds's play which cuts 'human beings out altogether' (p. 134) and the well-populated canvases of Plant's father. The contrast is, however, illusory. The elder Plant is not finally interested in the people he paints, only in composition; he, too, is a formalist, resisting all suggestions of self-disclosure. This is not surprising in view of his secret and criminal source of income. More seriously, his anti-semitism (much stronger in the 1942 version) and his loathing of 'development' are evidently unbalanced, disgusting as well as comic. He is thus a disturbing presence in the text, loathsome yet curiously sympathetic. His son inherits his father's defensiveness, but there is something else in his character which makes the younger Plant vulnerable to the three-pronged attack of Julia, Atwater and Lucy. *Work Suspended* is a study in the subversion of reserve, of defensiveness, social, verbal and personal, by the human element.

In the 1942 version, Plant outlines an interesting theory of characterization. 'The algebra of fiction,' he writes, 'must reduce its problems to symbols if they are to be soluble at all . . . There is no place in literature for a live man, solid and active' (quoted by Stannard, p. 496). The nearest a writer can come to putting 'life' into a work is by maintaining 'a kind of Dickensian menagerie', but Plant hopes to eschew such extravagance. Lucy, in particular, he insists, is presented in his text 'in the classic way', as 'a manageable abstraction'. Unfortunately, at least from his point of view, having replaced the astringent decencies of third-person narration with the structurally less formal processes of reminiscence, he cannot reduce himself to a formula in the same sort of way. When the narrator is also an actor in a narrative, lingering description, explanation and speculation are not so obviously the 'authorial' intrusions or indulgences they might otherwise seem. Plant is thus lured into saying more than is wise, notably when he recalls the moment of his falling in love:

it came without surprise; I had sensed it on its way, as an animal, still in profound darkness and surrounded by all the sounds of night, will lift its head, sniff, and know, inwardly, that dawn is near. (p. 163)

This is a risky piece of writing from Plant's point of view because it casually connects him with the Humboldt's Gibbon in London Zoo which, like Plant, dislikes being stared at, and refuses to perform in public, but which engages in private rituals at night, as 'exiled darkies, when their work is done . . . tread out the music of Africa in a vacant lot behind the drug-store' (p. 181). Perhaps there are similarly atavistic elements in Plant himself: Lucy significantly loves the animal and feeds it, Plant plays a mildly sadistic trick on it.

In a first-person narrative, then, life and presence, like personal feeling, put on the livery of the defence, disguise themselves as symbols, and so pass through the mind's defences into its well-policed imperial city, possibly with the connivance of elements within, and so make civilized authors sitting shots to the world. The danger is not so much in writing about oneself, as in the formal freedoms of reminiscence, which weaves elaborate narrative shapes across time, linking the present of the narration with the now of the writing, and setting up casual but telling connections between the events and feelings recalled and the hazardous associations of the creative art of writing.

Nor is an author like Plant vulnerable only when the subject is himself. Similar processes can operate in his relationships with other people. They are particularly evident in the account of Plant's relations with Julia and Atwater. Plant is plainly embarrassed by his treatment of Julia, and presumably anticipates his readers' seeing that embarrassment and his own ability (within limits) to acknowledge it. But even after Julia has given him the supremely unselfish present of cigars, he continues to regard her feelings for him as trivial in comparison with his own for Lucy. He fails to see that his 'resolve to force [his] friendship' (p. 163) on Lucy corresponds exactly with Julia's pursuit of himself, although her behaviour is better judged, more honourable, more mature than his own. He also fails to see how Atwater's attentions to him correspond with his to Lucy, and how Atwater's thick skin is a comic objectification of his own defensiveness. The chief difference between Atwater and men like Plant and Roger is that the insensitivity of the latter is a social skill acquired in the course of a male, upper-class education, and maintained by an artificial code of conduct, while Atwater's is a personal gift, prodigiously and solipsistically developed.

Atwater has several predecessors in Waugh's work – notably Corker in *Scoop*, and Grimes in *Decline and Fall*. He has the former's social ineptitude and the latter's monstrously mythic power: as the slayer of Plant's father, he is, after all, Plant's oedipal *alter ego* – a notion which Waugh would have regarded sceptically as a theory, but which he would have found amusing as a piece of symbolic algebra. But whereas Grimes was a figure out of the

Dickensian menagerie, there is an awful social realism about Atwater: he is the upper-class Englishman's nightmare – the vulgarian who cannot be embarrassed into accepting his place in the scheme of things. Yet he is a product of the same system – one suspects that his imperviousness to insult is a consequence of merciless bullying at school – and in the last paragraph of 'Postscript' (added in 1949) he becomes a portent: he is going to inherit the earth, or at any rate 'a large area of Germany'. He is thus in a curious way an historical figure, an awful warning to those whose smooth exploitation of the English class-system has misled them into making assumptions about its stability. He is also the means by which Plant, too, is historically placed. As one of the forces besieging the citadel of Plant's self-containment, and also as the embodiment of something inside as well as outside Plant's personality, Atwater helps us to see social and even political contradictions in Plant's defensiveness and vulnerability, contradictions which are far more interesting and complex than Roger's vulgar Marxist mouthings.

Lucy is the third of the forces threatening Plant's defences, and the one which most clearly has 'a Fifth Column among the garrison' (p. 131). Pregnant, well mannered, guileless, and not at all like Diana Guinness, she is a reminder in Plant's masculine world of naturalness and womanliness. His well-defended citadel is designed to resist the intrusions of death as well as those of love, yet even though Lucy's mother died giving birth to her, and she herself has a difficult labour, Plant is drawn to the 'lithe, chaste and unstudied nudity' of her mind (p. 170), as the civilized man is drawn to the innocent savage. She is cut off from Plant and his friends by a 'lack of shyness' which makes her unable to cope 'with the attack and defence, deception and exposure' which is their 'habitual intercourse' (p. 171). But Plant is not like his friends. While Roger is nonplussed at being unable to regard his pregnant wife 'in terms of ownership and use' (p. 173), Plant becomes obsessed with Lucy precisely because he *cannot* own or use her. His relationship with her seems to be a sign of his basic but unacknowledged niceness. This may also account for his relations with Julia and Atwater – for they, too, in different ways, are psychological savages, and if Plant finds himself unable to cope with them according to his established code of conduct, this may be because they threaten to show him his own unexpectedly innocent and vulnerable heart of darkness.

Work Suspended thus tells us more about its putative author than he realizes. Does it do the same about its real author? Waugh cannot be reductively identified with Plant any more than the women in the story can be identified with Diana Guinness and Laura Herbert. In any case the interesting question is whether this exploration of the personal and artistic dilemmas of a writer *like* himself amounts to a form of public self-questioning. To what extent were Waugh's own conservatism and reserve as stiff-necked and temperamental as Plant's? Is he signalling doubts about that self-assurance in the presence of folly and vice which had hitherto informed his writing? The implications of his quite startling change of style and narrative position are equally intriguing. The author of *Work Suspended* discloses a pleasure in rich writing which beguiles him in the same way as Lucy's loveliness beguiles his fictional narrator. But Plant's relationship with Lucy ends with the birth of her baby. It is a blind alley. We may also assume that Julia would have come back on the scene, possibly as the woman Plant was really going to fall in love with. It would have been interesting to see the effect of her unaffected passion on Waugh's prose. One thing, however, is clear: the authorial position is altogether less fixed in this story than it was in earlier works.

In the dedication of *Work Suspended* in 1942, Waugh wrote, 'the world in which and for which it was designed, has ceased to exist' (quoted in Stannard, p. 500); history had blundered in on his novel and rudely closed it down. But that closure was also a disclosure. Between 1942 and 1949 *Work Suspended* was transformed 'from a personal document to a more soberly "topical" allegory' (Stannard, p. 495). This generation of new meaning from without was not an accident. The original version described Plant's mind in terms of the ambiguous imperialist geography of the earlier novels which kept the civilized and the barbaric in constant tension. Plant's mental state was thus always full of historical and political implication. Consequently even if the imminent collapse of civilization made the undoing of John Plant and his friends of too little account for a serious novelist, they were still sufficiently alike to make the fragment as we have it an appropriate prelude to war, and its abandonment at the back of a drawer a striking way of getting things into proportion.

Throughout the summer and autumn of 1939, Waugh was much occupied by a slightly undignified scramble to find employment and to let his house. Eventually he was commisioned in the Royal Marines, spent a year in various home postings, and participated in an unsuccessful expedition to Dakar. He then joined Combined Operations, transferring to the Royal Horse Guards. He sailed to the Middle East in 1941 and took part in a night raid on Libya and the evacuation of Crete, after which he transferred back to the Marines, and wrote *Put Out More Flags* while sailing home.

At first sight this return to the world of Peter, Alastair and Basil looks like a retreat from the experimentation of *Work Suspended*, but this does the novel an injustice. In the Dedicatory Letter to Randolph Churchill, Waugh writes:

these pages . . . deal, mostly, with a race of ghosts, the survivors of the world we both knew ten years ago . . . where my imagination still fondly lingers. I find more food for thought in the follies of Basil Seal and Ambrose Silk, than in the sagacity of the higher command. These characters are no longer contemporary in sympathy; they were forgotten even before the war; but they lived on delightfully in holes and corners and, like everyone else, they have been disturbed in their habits by the rough intrusion of current history. (p. 7)

This says more than it seems to. The once up-to-date young author is now as outdated as his characters, but events have given those characters a new kind of fictive life. Waugh is still isolated, a provocative observer *sub specie aeternitatis* of folly and vice, smuggling barbarian excitements into the imperial city or discovering them there, but now he is isolated by nostalgia for a lost paradise, and he has a changed audience to arrange his thoughts for. *Put Out More Flags* engages in adjustments of perspective and technique which are a considered response to history. It is the product of, and a judgement upon, great events.

One of its most telling innovations is its social realism, its references to politics, to the Russian attack on Finland, to Chamberlain and Hore-Belisha, to the Ministry of Information and the armed forces. *Vile Bodies* presented a cartoon version of politics at a time when 'the next war' was only a journalistic catch-phrase, while the fictional histories of Azania and Ishmaelia signalled only limited connections with real events. In *Put Out More Flags* Basil's wanderings along 'the outer fringe of contemporary history' (p. 148) take him from fictional Azania into Spain, Czechoslovakia and Mexico; each of the chapters is linked to actual events between September 1939 and the summer of 1940; and the bland prognostications of Sir Joseph Mainwaring are simply wrong in fact. *Put Out More Flags* is not uniformly realistic – if it were it could not have contained the purely literary fun of Mr Rampole's last hours of freedom – but history insistently intrudes and modifies the note of stylish detachment it shares with the pre-war novels.

The change is particularly marked in its use of linguistic registers – the jargon of the military, for example. Waugh is still a parodist, approaching the dead metaphors of the officers' mess like a Russian Formalist at the top of his defamiliarizing bent:

The first time that Captain Mayfield had asked him, 'Are you in the picture, Trumpington?' he supposed him to mean, was he personally conspicuous. He crouched at the time water-logged to the knees, in a ditch; he had, at the suggestion of Mr Smallwood – the platoon commander – ornamented his steel helmet with bracken. 'No, sir,' he had said, stoutly. (p. 128)

But Waugh also uses military vocabulary with a new kind of seriousness. The embarkation fiasco, for which Cedric Lyne gets the blame, is both funny and informative. Waugh's thorough grasp of the usages, linguistic and practical, of Army life, gives it the realism of a documentary film, while his technically exact description of the military action in Norway invests Cedric's death with a gravity new to his fiction.

The race of ghosts in *Put Out More Flags* is thus involved in more complex and riskier relationships than those represented in the earlier novels. Basil in particular is no longer surrounded by algebraic symbols but by people with real lives to live – his mistress, Angela Lyne, his sister's neighbours, his family, his friends, and the artistic coterie of which Ambrose Silk is the most important member – and his action on their lives is catalytic in a thoroughly disturbing fashion.

Waugh's treatment of Angela is the most important technical development in the book. He introduces her with the detail and explanation of a major character in a traditional novel, adopting the timeworn device of describing her as a stranger might see her, before outlining her real history, thoughts and feelings. Initially she seems no more than a glamorous presence, like Margot in *Decline and Fall*.

Her smartness was individual; she was plainly not one of those who scrambled to buy the latest gadget in the few breathless weeks between its first appearance and the inundation of the cheap markets of the world with its imitations; her person was a record and criticism of succeeding fashions, written as it were, year after year, in one clear and characteristic fist. (p. 25)

But these well-formed sentences are the correlate of Angela's style, establishing an unspoken affinity between character and author, not least in the word 'fist' (slang for handwriting): Angela and Waugh are alike in the unexpected toughness with which each individualizes what they record and criticize. However, this apparent affinity is disrupted by Waugh's moral vocabulary. First he smacks Angela in the face with his own 'fist' by describing her relationship with Basil as

a standing, frightful example of the natural qualities of man and woman, of their basic aptitude to fuse together . . . so that the least censorious were chilled by the spectacle and recoiled saying, 'Really, you know, there's something rather squalid about those two.' (pp. 26–7)

He then describes Basil boasting in his cups and Angela waiting 'her turn to strike, hard and fierce, at his conceit', but Basil talks her down as he gets drunker and eventually comes 'stupidly away' (p. 27). Finally Waugh moves into a stream-of-consciousness evocation of Angela's thoughts, literate and deadly, as they move longingly towards her own freedom and Basil's death. Waugh was unpersuaded by the claims of psychoanalysis, but no writer handles love and death, the great themes of Freudian speculation, more suavely or persuasively.

The story of this love affair is told in Waugh's accustomed manner; the phrase about Angela's talking like a man recurs like a refrain; the wit informing her 'haphazard trail of phrase and association' (p. 29) on her journey through France later degenerates into drunken meanderings – 'she said to herself as loudly as though to someone sitting opposite on the Empire day-bed, "Maginot Line – Angela Lyne – both lines of least resistance" and laughed at her joke until the tears came and suddenly she found herself weeping in earnest' (p. 151). Basil brings her round and she stages a remarkable social comeback at Peter's wedding; but Basil goes on to betray Ambrose, and Angela to behave with crushing coldness towards Cedric and Nigel. She is the most intelligent of Waugh's women characters, and she has an authentic moral sense. The quotation which serves as her comment on the death of a betrayed husband – 'The dog it was that died' – is proof of both; but her 'happy ending' is chilling. She and Basil are united by death far more seriously than Basil and Prudence were. The comparison, touched on during Angela's meditation on the train, is part of the later novel's meaning.

This appalling love story is played out contrapuntally with Basil's other adventures, each of which ends up by turning serious – even the funny game of letting Basil loose among his sister's neighbours. This is a reworking of an earlier short story, 'An Englishman's Home', in which retired members of the pious and honourable classes are tricked by two brothers pretending to be property developers. Basil's game is less genteel. It is also even more serious than his depradations among the Azanians. Azania had always been a fictional country, but the England of *Put Out More Flags* was wholly present to its original readers: in effect, Basil cuckolds a 'real' soldier training for a 'real' war. And it is precisely this 'realism' that makes this part of *Put Out More Flags* much more interesting than 'An Englishman's Home'. The Connolly children (so named as a further joke at Cyril Connolly's expense) are more than a domestic species of the Earl of Ngumo's drunken soldiery descending on the civilized order of 'benevolent, companionable people' (p. 113). They signify the breakdown, in wartime conditions, of established class relationships. They are proletarian Atwaters, let loose among the retired administrators of the Empire.

Something of Waugh's intentions here is revealed in the entry in his diary for 10 October 1939:

A Red Cross flag day. It seems supremely ridiculous that while an essentially charitable enterprise – giving refuge to threatened children – should be financed by taxes and enforced by the police, the provision of medical service for the army should be thought a suitable field for private charity. (*Diaries*, p. 445)

A touch of this censoriousness colours the descriptions of Basil's victims. Waugh notes their 'carefully limited families' (p. 114), and implies that their benevolence is limited too. They feed the birds in winter, 'with the crumbs from the dining-room table' – an ironic evocation of the words of the Syro-Phoenician woman to Jesus (Matthew 15: 27) – and they see 'to it that no old person in the village [goes] short of coal'. But the system of piety and honour, by which the 'tribute of Empire flowed gently into the agricultural countryside, tithe barns were converted into village halls, the boy scouts had a new bell tent and the district nurse a new motor car' – this description is lifted almost unchanged from 'An Englishman's Home' – cannot cope with the turbulent tribal life of the northern slums.

The seriousness of the theme of class in *Put Out More Flags* is particularly evident in its treatment of money. In the earlier works, class was understood in terms of speech and manner. Money was an additional asset, but its acquisition and possession were matters of luck. In *Put Out More Flags*, on the other hand, class is perceived as the settled possession of wealth and the complex solidarity and mutual competitiveness of institutionalized privilege. Although he hated Marxism as fiercely as psychoanalysis, Waugh never defended social inequality in terms of the merits of those who did well out of it. His attitudes are finely woven into his account of how 'three rich women [think] first and mainly of Basil Seal' (p. 9), and particularly the opening section in which Barbara Sothill faces the problem of her evacuees.

Barbara is in the story to be liked. (As with all the upper-class women in the novel, she is more astute than her partner – even Lady Seal has the edge over Sir Joseph in this respect.) Yet Waugh adds some slightly sinister touches to his account of her. She can see Hitler, for example, only as 'a small and envious mind, a meanly ascetic mind, a creature of the conifers . . . plotting the destruction of her home. It was for Malfrey,' we are told, 'that she loved her prosaic and slightly absurd husband' (pp. 9–10), who, Waugh adds later, was 'at heart . . . misanthropic and gifted with that sly, sharp instinct for self-preservation that passes for wisdom among the rich' (p. 13). Then there is the theme of ownership, worked deftly into the account of Barbara's encounters with the evacuees. She cannot address them as individuals and their mistrust makes her 'determined not to be cut *in her own village*' (my italics), so she invites them into the grounds of Malfrey, but even this generosity is misunderstood. '. . . The idea of inviting us into the park,' says the chief mother, when Barbara leaves. 'You'd think the place belonged to her the way she goes on'. All this is harmless enough, though the women come off well: parks in towns *are* public places. But the final touch in this run of references to ownership undoes any suggestion of blandness in Waugh's handling of the theme. Recalling Basil's theft of his mother's emeralds in *Black Mischief*, Barbara says, '. . . that would never have happened if there'd been a war *of our own* for him to go to' (my italics) (p. 16). Great historical events, it seems, are as liable to enclosure by the rich as the common land of England once was, particularly when it lay adjacent to their splendid houses.

It is among these privileged proprietors of 'England' and 'the war', however, that Waugh's imagination fondly lingers, and we are bound to ask whether it does not do so self-indulgently, at least in the cases of Peter and Alastair. Alastair's characterization is the easier to defend. Putting himself through it because he overdid things in a decade of parties is of a piece with his hangdog letter to Paul Pennyfeather after the Bollinger binge those many years ago. Peter's naïvety cannot be similarly justified, however, because the idea that Margot ran an international vice ring had to be quietly dropped after *Vile Bodies* and with it that air of slightly soiled innocence with which the young Peter Beste-Chetwynde was once invested. A less interesting innocence replaces it, but not an intrinsically inadequate characterization. Yet even if the old Alastair and the new Peter are acceptable as characters, we may still ask whether what the Dedicatory Letter calls the Churchillian renaissance – the transition from the England of Appeasement and the Phoney War to the embattled Britain of 1940 – is adequately represented by Waugh's turning well-born young sybarites into little boys eager for a fight and their wives into wisely indulgent mothers delighted to join in the game.

The theme of immaturity, however, is as carefully worked into the text as the theme of ownership, and the catalytic element is again Basil.

'Don't be a chump,' said Basil, relapsing, as he often did with Barbara, into the language of the schoolroom. 'I'll fix it for you.'
'Swank. Chump yourself. Double chump.' (p. 54)

Doris Connolly has a primitive intuition into what this is all about. When Barbara protests that she and Basil are not lovers but brother and sister, Doris, 'her pig eyes dark with the wisdom of the slums', replies, 'Ah, but you fancy him, don't you? I saw.' (p. 88). Doris is wrong, but only because Basil and Barbara are narcissists and are startlingly alike: when they kiss, 'Narcissus [greets] Narcissus from the watery depths' (p. 87) of two pairs of blue eyes. All of the Metroland characters are similarly absorbed – in themselves, or in each other, or at best in 'their' war. None of them sees the history that has intruded on their lives. Basil is as wrong about events as Sir Joseph. Waugh may have endowed his race of ghosts with a sort of natural grace, but this no more amounts to an authorial endorsement of their point of view than his conviction that great houses should remain in private hands amounts to an endorsement of Freddy's way of making 'an agreeable sum of money' (p. 141) out of turning Malfrey over to the Yeomanry.

But what point of view could possibly encompass the rough intrusion of history into the world of the novel? ' "It is an evil thing we are fighting," [the Prime Minister] had said' (p. 9) – yet only one character, Ambrose Silk, knows how evil. Aesthete, homosexual and Jew, Ambrose labours under the triple curse of a sense of beauty, a sense of love and a sense of history – not the history of

England only, but of his people, of his kind and of the world. He is in consequence the only character in the novel with a function to match that of Basil. Together they constitute its moral heart.

Ambrose represents both the failure of aestheticism and the significance of its claims. Once he dwelt in Arcadia, a peaceful Limbo of conversation (that 'most exquisite and exacting of the arts' – p. 59), of 'Diaghilev . . . Lovat Frazer rhyme sheets . . . Jean Cocteau . . . Gertrude Stein . . . Montparnasse Negroes . . . fashionable photographers, stage sets for Cochrane, Cedric Lyne and his Neapolitan grottoes' (p. 43). But this 'primrose path' led 'downhill', and to save his soul alive Ambrose aligned himself with the literary Left, with Parsnip and Pimpernell (W. H. Auden and Christopher Isherwood) who then upped and sailed for America in the spring of 1939. So when war breaks out he is stuck in the same 'galley' as Poppet Green and her friends, listening to their excuses for Parsnip and Pimpernell and remembering how earlier artists answered the call to arms – Socrates, Xenophon, Virgil, Horace, Cervantes, Milton, and even poor George IV. Finally isolated, he develops his theory that art should be 'cenobitic' – the work of 'lonely men of few books and fewer pupils' (p. 176) like the scholars of China – rather than 'conventual' – 'of value to the community' (p. 186). This sad fantasy is grimly fulfilled in his own case, when he is isolated in the wet wastes of Ireland in wartime, and tragically in Cedric's as he walks to his death, thinking Ambrose's thoughts without knowing it. Aestheticism is as inadequate to the challenge of evil in *Put Out More Flags* as the self-absorption of shadows more fashionable than Ambrose and Cedric.

But Ambrose has a problem more deep-seated than his aestheticism – his homosexuality. 'Here is the war, offering a new deal for everyone,' he thinks; 'I alone bear the weight of my singularity' (p. 61). But he also knows that it is history, not his 'nature', that has disabled him. (He thinks of heroic homosexuals – Leonardo, the Spartans, Saladin, the Knights Templar.) Moreover, he knows what the war is all about *because* of his sexuality, because of his love for Hans. That is why the scramble for jobs and the appropriation and personalizing of the war disgust him:

. . . all war is nonsense, thought Ambrose. I don't care about their war. It's got nothing on me. But if, thought Ambrose, I was one of these people, if I were not a cosmopolitan, Jewish pansy, if I were not all that the Nazis mean when they talk about 'degenerates', if I were not a single, sane individual, if I were part of a herd . . . Gawd strike me pink, thought Ambrose . . . I'd set about killing and stampeding the other herd as fast and as hard as I could. Lord love a duck, thought Ambrose, there wouldn't be any animals nosing around for suitable jobs in *my* herd. (p. 73)

This meditation concludes the first chapter. The second begins:

Winter set in hard. Poland was defeated; east and west prisoners rolled away to slavery. (p. 74)

But if Ambrose is right, how is it that Basil is allowed so cruelly to victimize him? An answer to this can be found in the novel's epigraphs. The first is both celebratory and valedictory. *Put Out More Flags* is Captain Waugh's farewell party. It is in that spirit that he has Basil paint a ginger moustache on to Poppet Green's head of Aphrodite, and invites us to laugh at the posturings of the literary Left, the absurdities of the Ministry of Information, and Basil's mischief-making – his exploitation of the Connollys, his destruction of Colonel Plumb's career and Mr Rampole's domestic arrangements, and his dispatch of Ambrose to Ireland disguised as a priest. It is in that spirit that he describes Malfrey in the kind of prose that Lucy aroused in the narrator of *Work Suspended*, that he marries Peter off to a wonderful girl, and arranges for his favourite characters to join his own unit; it is in that spirit that he allows the poor booby, Sir Joseph, to be centre-stage and 'bang right' when the party ends.

It would be reductive, however, to see the novel merely in terms of the first epigraph. It also addresses the problem of drowning a great injustice in the world by the sword. In 1937, reviewing a book about the First World War, Waugh wrote of 'the vile impertinence of assuring our elders that fighting is on the whole rather fun' (*Essays*, p. 201), but he also warned against taking a too negative view of war. 'War', he argued, 'is an absolute loss, but it admits of degrees; it is very bad to fight, but it is worse to lose' (*Essays*, p. 200). He accepted, however, that its 'spiritual consequences' (*Essays*, p. 201) were deplorable – 'the pollution of truth, the deterioration of human character in prolonged unnatural stress, the emergence of the bully and the cad, the obliteration of chivalry'. *Put Out More Flags* includes all these elements, and in particular it tells the story of how Basil Seal, bully and cad, comes fully into his own alongside swashbuckling schoolboys like Peter and Alastair. His caddishness is exactly specified in the enumeration of his motives for helping Ambrose escape: he resents Colonel Plumb's 'getting all the credit and all the fun' (p. 193); he dislikes 'being on the side of the law' (pp. 193–4); he is conscious that Ambrose might disclose 'Basil's share in editing *Monument to a Spartan*' (p. 194); and he has 'from long association an appreciable softness of disposition towards Ambrose'. 'These considerations, in that order of importance, worked in Basil's mind.' (ibid.) Of the younger characters Basil has the last word. 'There's only one serious occupation for a chap now, that's killing Germans. I have an idea I shall rather enjoy that' (Epilogue). In every horrible respect he is bang right.

As, indeed, Ambrose could have told him. The epigraphs were, after all, translated from the Chinese sages so admired by Ambrose, and only he has the wit and wisdom to appreciate how their incompatibility with each other and the cenobitic ideal encompasses a terrible truth.

Waugh was 39 in October 1942. It had been a 'good year', he wrote (*Diaries*, p. 530). Laura had had another child, he had published a successful book, he had lived well and he had rejoined the Special Services Brigade. In the following year, however, his father died, his unit sailed for North Africa without him, and he was required to resign from the Brigade. He was 'so unpopular as to be unemployable' (*Diaries*, p. 532) – his superiors feared he would be shot by his own men in battle. Early in 1944 he obtained permission to take indefinite leave to write a novel – *Brideshead Revisited: The Sacred and Profane Memories of Captain Charles Ryder*.

It was a first-person narrative and therefore a risky project. In the 1945 version, Charles Ryder writes:

These memories are the memorials and pledges of the vital hours of a lifetime. These hours of afflatus in the human spirit, the springs of art, are, in their mystery, akin to the epochs of history, when a race which for centuries has lived content, unknown, behind its own frontiers ... will, for a generation or two, stupefy the world, bring to birth and nurture a teeming brood of genius, droop ... fall, but leave behind a record of new rewards won for all mankind ...

The human soul enjoys these rare, classic periods, but, apart from them, we are seldom single or unique; we keep company ... with a hoard of abstractions and reflexions and counterfeits of ourselves ... till we get the chance to drop unnoticed ... pause, breathe freely and take our bearings, or to push ahead, out-distance our shadows ... so that, when at length they catch up with us, they look at one another askance, knowing we have a secret we shall never share. (pp. 214–5)

The novel was written at a similar moment of isolation in Waugh's own life. It helped him to take his bearings, to refresh himself on memories – Oxford, friendship with Alastair Graham, life at Madresfield and Mells, wine, food, travel, sexual intoxication and religious conversion. From another point of view it was itself like one of the obscure races Charles describes. It burst through the frontiers of reserve, teeming with new characters, incidents, settings and even meals, and then slipped back into obscurity, for Waugh was to write nothing like it again. Above all it teemed with words, with metaphors, descriptions and meditations. The long speeches of Charles's father, cunning, eccentric and lonely, are fluent, inventive and psychologically penetrating; those of Anthony Blanche witty, sinister, wise, menacing and exquisitely understated in their attitude towards Charles. And, in spite of the doubts to which Waugh refers in his 1960 Preface, Julia Flyte's lament about mortal sin and the soliloquy of the dying Lord Marchmain are at least as impressive.

The chief source of this linguistic abundance is the movement of Charles's mind, enraptured by his memories of the Flyte family and the grace with which they possessed their secular inheritance. Other, less beguiling kinds of language – the slovenliness of Hooper, the comic infelicities of Army usage, the prosiness of Jaspar, the self-regarding archness of Mr Samgrass, the shallow worldliness of Rex Mottram, the fashionable insincerity of Celia Mulcaster – dramatize contemporary social tensions, notably the distinctions between the Ryder and Flyte families, and the threat posed to both by Hooper – the Common Man awarded the King's Commission. Academic parasitism is well represented by Mr Samgrass, while Rex brilliantly personifies the plutocratic coarseness of the pre-war Conservative Party. But all this is no more than a vehicle for grander explorations of values in a fallen world. The meditative temper of the older Charles's prose (so different from the younger Charles's agnostic common sense) makes even strawberries and a bottle of Chateau Peyraguey seem (in the words of the dust-jacket of the first edition) 'at once romantic and eschatological' (*Essays*, p. 288). In *Work Suspended* and *Put Out More Flags*, underlying images of a struggle between civilization and barbarism made both psychological and historical change a dialectical process, but in *Brideshead Revisited* competing value-systems simply cancel each other out. The one 'historical' event in the main action, the General Strike, barely disturbs the old routine. The major forces for change are self-betrayal and decay. Brideshead may be requisitioned by a conscript Army, its fountain dry and litter-filled, its rooms vandalized, but it is not the People's War which brings it to this pass. By 1939, the house and what it represents have worked their own destruction. The Army simply moves in later, like Indians taking possession of the mausoleums Charles sketches in Mexico.

Brideshead symbolizes many things, but most obviously architecture, the art which for Waugh required and expressed the triumph of civilization over barbarism. In the first version of the novel, Charles writes of architecture as 'the highest achievement of man' (p. 215) and recalls thinking of 'men as something much less than the buildings they had made and inhabited'. His vocation is to make records of fine houses before their demolition, a process he describes as the 'jungle closing in' as it closes in on the 'gutted palaces and cloisters embowered with weed' which he draws in Mexico. Colonial Mexico, Waugh believed, was 'a land of magnificent architecture and prosperous industry . . . of civil peace and high culture . . . [which was] broken by . . . dictatorship . . . revolution and civil war' (*Essays*, p. 250). But the sustained meditation in *Brideshead Revisited* on the verse from the Book of Lamentations, '*Quomodo sedet sola civitas*' – 'How doth the city sit solitary' – is depoliticized. Brideshead is Tony Last's City, derelict and abandoned, but instead of invasion by the armies of Babylon, which was the fate of Jerusalem in Lamentations, what we witness is the deadlier attrition of decay.

Brideshead also stands for love and its betrayal. It is more than the Flytes' home: it would have been Charles's had he married Julia, and its dereliction in Prologue and Epilogue stands for the failure of their passion. The chapel, Lady Marchmain's wedding present, becomes a ghastly *memento matrimonii*, and the fountain a trysting place for shadow lovers only. Brideshead is finally sterile. The interaction of Catholicism with the personalities of Lord and Lady Marchmain turn their eldest son into a religious obsessive capable of marriage only to the spiteful Beryl; Sebastian into a lonely homosexual, a failed pagan, an alcoholic and a sponger; Julia into Rex's faithless wife whose resurrected conscience destroys the love of her life; and Cordelia into a plain, do-gooding spinster. In some respects *The Waste Land* finds a truer reflection in *Brideshead Revisited* than in *A Handful of Dust*.

Except, of course, for the ripe, abundant prose. But words betray those who let them become entangled with their emotions. 'Thank God I think I am beginning to acquire a style' (*Diaries*, p. 560), Waugh wrote as he was working on the novel. When it was published, however, it was greeted variously with malice, curiosity, amusement and dismay. It seemed too ornate. Although he himself was frustrated at not being free to compare them in greater detail, the sexual scenes involving Celia and Julia were thought ill judged; the deathbed repentance of Lord Marchmain was condemned as propagandist and ridiculous; and the intimacy between Sebastian and Charles evoked memories in those who knew them of Waugh's friendship with Alastair Graham. He had apparently put his own seduction by the English upper class, and a singularly snobbish kind of Catholicism, on public record. Charles might write of the artist having a secret which no one else may share. It seemed to many that Waugh had let his secret seep through his prose and stain his pages.

Sensitive to these criticisms, he twice revised the novel. The 1960 edition was divided into three books, not two, and substantial cuts were made to descriptive and meditative passages. There is an element of civilized disingenuousness in the Preface to this edition, not least in its explanation of how the novel came to be written in war-time, but Waugh's embarrassment was probably less personal and more professional than has been thought. He was more likely to feel self-conscious about publicizing his gluttony than vices higher in the catalogue of grave sins, and more embarrassed by an ill judged conceit than a compromising autobiographical reference. In any case his excisions leave the essential problem of the novel unresolved, which is that to many people it seems both too worldly in its treatment of religion and too religious in its treatment of the world.

One aspect of this problem is Lady Marchmain. Nancy Mitford asked Waugh if he was 'on Lady Marchmain's side' (*Letters*, p. 196). This is a legitimate question, for Lady Marchmain seems to be an emotionally insecure woman, formidably well defended and seriously inhibited; in short, to have a typically manipulative personality. She presumably speaks better than she knows when she says, 'Any failure in my children is my failure' (p. 162). Her beauty, wealth and social standing have made it far too easy for her to get her way, and she is correspondingly devastated when she fails to do so. The type is a familiar one, Thackeray's Lady Castlewood in *The History of Henry Esmond* and Pen's mother in *Pendennis* being notable examples. But Nancy Mitford's question could be asked of Thackeray also. Clearly, if Waugh cannot see his character's personality type, his entire project is at risk since Lady Marchmain's manipulative behaviour extends above all to her religion, which is only confirmed for her when other people submit to it at her bidding. Yet she is the source of the Catholicism of all the principal characters in the novel. Is the stream of Faith in effect poisoned at its head?

A related problem is Charles's rhetoric. In his reply to Nancy Mitford, Waugh calls Charles 'dim' and 'a bad painter' – Anthony applies the fatal word 'charm' to Charles's work – but while the story he tells, as Waugh points out, is not 'his', its effects on his point of view are constitutive of his way of telling it. Does *Brideshead Revisited*, then, attempt to seduce the reader as Lady Marchmain attempts to seduce Charles – 'circling, approaching, retreating, feinting' (p. 132), playing a verbal equivalent of the child's game 'grandmother's steps'? Sebastian gives further grounds for anxiety when he says he believes in the Christmas story because it's 'a lovely idea' (p. 84); when Charles protests, Sebastian insists. 'That's how I believe.' Is there not a suggestion here (in spite of the careful use of 'how' and not 'why') that it might be no bad thing to find oneself charmed into the Faith by engaging simplicity such as this?

In this and the next chapter, however, there are strong counter-suggestions to such apparently reductive aestheticism. They are contained in three casual but related references to primitive peoples. The most notorious of these is a passage about the brothers of Lady Marchmain who were killed in the First World War. They are described as

> set apart from their fellows, garlanded victims, devoted to the sacrifice. These men must die to make a world for Hooper; they were the aborigines, vermin by right of law, to be shot off at leisure so that things might be safe for the travelling salesman, with his polygonal pince-nez, his fat wet hand-shake, his grinning dentures. (p. 134)

The snobbery here (Charles's or Mr Samgrass's, it is hard to tell which) has diverted attention from the fact that the passage compares Lady Marchmain's brothers to those ultimate victims of imperialist atrocity, the aboriginal peoples of Australia. This comparison is reinforced by the description of Sebastian's grim-faced uncle whose writings Mr Samgrass has edited, as 'a man of the woods and caves . . . the repository of the harsh traditions of a people at war with their environment' (p. 133). The graciousness of the younger Flytes, it seems, has descended to them from their Protestant, not their Catholic forebears. That is why Sebastian seems to Charles like 'a happy and harmless . . . Polynesian' (p. 122) and his mother's religion like 'the grim invasion of trader, administrator, missionary and tourist' (p. 123). Catholicism is thus represented on the one hand as primitive and rebarbative, on the other as the ally of imperialist oppression. Hooper and the Faith, travelling salesman and gracious young aristocrat, conquering imperialist and noble savage, do not compose themselves into a simple allegory.

Even more disturbing is Charles's suggestion that there might be some 'blaze' on Lady Marchmain and her children, marking them out 'for destruction by other ways than war'. Here some fundamental Catholic notions become relevant. Knox writes:

> The Catholic notion of God's relation to the universe is summed up once for all in Our Lord's statement that no sparrow can fall on the ground without our Heavenly Father; there can be no event, however insignificant, however apparently fortuitous, however cruel in its bearing on the individual, which does not demand, here and now, the concurrence of Divine Power. (*The Belief of Catholics*, p. 76)

Everything that happens – the extinction of a whole race or of a single family – is providential. At the end of the novel, therefore, Charles discerns a providential concurrence in 'the fierce little human tragedy' (p. 332) which he has narrated, for it has led to the relighting of 'a beaten-copper lamp of deplorable design' so that Mass can be said for conscript soldiers in time of war. No matter that the terrible beauty of the chant *Quomodo sedet sola civitas* has yielded to Army bugles sounding 'Pick-em-up, pick-em-up, hot potatoes': mortal beauty has only a modest place in the divine plan – people are much more than the buildings they temporarily inhabit. Even Hooper.

But the working out of a tragedy along such punitive lines only compounds the problem for many readers. It seems perverse to develop the case for Catholicism in terms of the allure of the Flyte family on the one hand *and* its nemesis on the other, to appropriate both romance and eschatology for Waugh's religion. Glamour and style are deployed, it seems, to attract the customers (Knox uses 'The Shop Window' metaphor in *The Belief of Catholics*), and then a harsh, life-denying fable is developed to show (in the words of the 1945 dust-jacket) 'that the human spirit, redeemed, can survive all disasters'. But there is no contradiction here: the point Waugh wishes to make is that Catholicism can indeed have it both ways because, though distinct, the natural and the supernatural are inseparable. On this point, Knox quotes Hebrews 12: 22 – 'You are come to Mount Sion, and to the city of the living God . . .' – and adds, 'the supernatural is already with us . . . the two worlds are perfectly distinct, but they intersect' (pp. 178–9).

This intersection applies to the whole of ordinary human experience. Even charm can be taken up into the supernatural order. Again, we can turn to Knox for an explanation:

There is among Catholic saints a familiarity which seems to raise this world to the level of eternity. There is among Catholic sinners a familiarity which seems (to non-Catholic eyes) to degrade eternity of the level of this world . . . For good or for evil, the ordinary, easy-going Catholic pays far less tribute to . . . [reverence] than a Protestant . . . No traveller fails to be struck, or perhaps shocked, by the 'irreverence' or 'naturalness' . . . of Catholic children . . . the Catholic takes the truths of religion for granted, whereas the non-Catholic unconsciously behaves as if there were a spell which would be broken if he treated his religion with familiarity; he might wake up suddenly, and find himself alone. (pp. 180–81)

Waugh found this attitude of holy irreverence among Catholics particularly appealing, especially when associated with the upper-class nonchalance of his friends at Mells; but, though praying for pigs and telling whoppers to would-be converts like Rex are thoroughly 'Catholic' ways of behaving, they are not central to Waugh's sense of how the natural and the supernatural intersect. To approach this, we need to consider Julia and Sebastian, Catholic sinner and Catholic saint.

Julia's sin is 'mortal' – it is a changeling in the cradle of her dead baby. But everything that happens, even sin, requires the concurrence of Divine Power: even adulterers live in the presence of the supernatural. When Julia registers dismay at how completely Charles has forgotten Sebastian, his reply – 'He was the forerunner' (p. 288) – is implicitly blasphemous, for if Sebastian was the forerunner like John the Baptist, Julia is Christ. Perhaps to extinguish this implied parallel she at once suggests that she might only be a forerunner too, prompting a passing thought in Charles:

perhaps all our loves are merely hints and symbols; vagabond-language scrawled on gate-posts and paving-stones along the weary road that others have tramped before us; perhaps you and I are types . . . snatching a glimpse now and then of the shadow which turns the corner always a pace or two ahead of us. (pp. 288–9)

Unwittingly, the poor agnostic has hit upon a truth: in Catholic teaching all the good things of creation, even unlawful love, point to the *summum bonum*, to the Beatific Vision Itself. Charles's idyll with Sebastian at Brideshead was an anticipatory sign of more than his passion for Julia: it was a type in the strict New Testament sense of Heaven itself. And Julia, too, is a preliminary presence in his life before he too becomes a Catholic. God and his Providence intersect even with her little, mad sin.

They intersect also with suffering. Suffering, in Catholic thought, is a condition of helplessness, of being in evil without being evil. The principle is enunciated in his inimitably charmless manner by Bridey, when he expresses the hope that Sebastian is a dipsomaniac, because that would simply be 'a great misfortune . . . There's nothing *wrong* with being a physical wreck you know' (p. 157). Bridey is in thrall to notions of 'moral obligation', and cannot, therefore, see what Cordelia recognizes, that Sebastian's condition is more than an excuse: it is a means of sanctification. Listening to her account of Sebastian's last days in Africa, Charles says, '. . . I suppose he doesn't suffer?'

'Oh, yes, I think he does [Cordelia answers]. One can have no idea what the suffering may be, to be maimed as he is – no dignity, no power of will. No one is ever holy without suffering . . . It's the spring of love . . .' (pp. 294–5)

These remarks complement her earlier explanation of her mother's deplorable effect on other people:

'I got on best with her of any of us, but I don't believe I ever really loved her. Not as she wanted or deserved . . .

'You didn't like her. I sometimes think when people wanted to hate God they hated mummy . . .

'. . . she was saintly but she wasn't a saint. No one could really hate a saint, could they? They can't really hate God either. When they want to hate Him and his Saints they have to find something like themselves and pretend it's God and hate that . . .' (p. 212–3)

This distinction between being saintly and being a saint resolves Nancy Mitford's problem. Sebastian is lovable; bound to the stake of his suffering, of his compulsion, he becomes a saint, like the martyr and homoerotic icon after whom he is named. Lady

Marchmain suffers too, but she is not lovable – that is her tragedy. Waugh was therefore quite justified in denying to Nancy Mitford that he was on Lady Marchmain's side. It would seem, on the contrary, that he set Lady Marchmain as a trap for the unwary reader. Being saintly, she provides us with an excuse for hating Catholicism. So, if we choose to let it, does the novel's prose.

Yet Waugh went on to assure Nancy Mitford that, although he wasn't on Lady Marchmain's side, God was. Destructive as her behaviour might be, it is not sinful. Cordelia's remark about finding something like oneself to hate in God's place reminds Charles of an earlier remark of Cara's, that when people hate with great energy, 'it is something in themselves they are hating' (p. 99). And Lady Marchmain hates, skilled as she is at hiding it. During the second of her talks with Charles, when she rebukes him for helping Sebastian to drink, she reveals herself as the greatest hater in the novel, and if Cara is right this means she must unconsciously hate herself. Her behaviour is thus as compulsive as her son's, and as deeply humiliating. Once we have got beyond the temptation to hate her in return, therefore, we may see her as maimed like Sebastian, less holy than he is but more fruitful. The manipulative *grande dame* is not, after all, the source of the novel's Catholicism, but she is its principal intermediary: 'the book', Waugh wrote in reply to Nancy Mitford, 'is about God' (*Letters*, p. 196); poor, hate-driven Lady Marchmain is his instrument.

Brideshead Revisited, Waugh wrote to his agent, 'is steeped in theology' (*Letters*, p. 188). A careful examination of Catholic principle certainly explains its complex literary strategy, but it does not necessarily establish its satisfactoriness as a narrative. Getting Lady Marchmain into focus leaves unresolved the problem posed by Lord Marchmain's death-bed conversion, on which the entire action hinges. The Flyte family is in important respects drawn from life. The chapel at Brideshead is taken from that at Madresfield, home of the Lygons, whose father had to live abroad like Lord Marchmain (though for different reasons). The death-bed scene is also based on fact. In the autumn of 1943 Hubert Duggan, a lapsed Catholic convert and stepson of Lord Curzon, was dying. He was divorced, and apparently thought that it would be a betrayal of the woman he

loved 'to profess repentance of his life with her' (*Diaries*, p. 552).
Waugh, however, consulted priests, and eventually Duggan
accepted absolution, was annointed *in extremis* and crossed himself,
as Lord Marchmain does in the novel. But writing of Catholics was
like writing about the Pie-wie in *A Handful of Dust*: Waugh
presented a real picture of people he had met, and most of his readers
simply did not believe him.

But there is a deeper problem. Lord Marchmain's repentance is
not miraculous; it involves no suspension of the laws of nature; but
it does violate a fundamental law in classical literary theory – it
winds up a plot with a simple change of mind by one of the principal
characters. In other words it is an example 'of deplorable design' –
just like the sanctuary lamp in Brideshead chapel. But that lamp is
the sign of God's Real Presence in the world of the novel, and Lord
Marchmain's repentance similarly signifies the triumph of eschatology over romance, and for that matter, over design and every
other imaginable human value. *Brideshead Revisited*, after all, is
'about God', and God is not a respecter of the norms of art. He
cannot be reduced to a term in the algebra of the novel, like a
character in one of John Plant's detective novels, nor does he turn up
in the right place, like a card in one of Mrs Rattery's games of
Patience. On the contrary his entry into the scheme of things cannot
be other than a scandal.

CHAPTER FOUR

Exiles:
Scott-King's Modern Europe,
the short stories, *The Loved One*, *Helena*
and *The Ordeal of Gilbert Pinfold*

Waugh did not return to active service. When he finished *Brideshead Revisited*, he joined Randolph Churchill on a mission to Yugoslavia. He found much to disturb him there; his Croatian fellow-Catholics faced a grim, uncertain future, and he was moved by the plight of a party of Jewish refugees. On his return home he was quickly demobilized. The election in 1945 of a Labour Government alarmed him. It seemed like a victory for semi-Marxist notions of progress which threatened personal freedom and civilized life. He thought of state planning as inept and the idea of a prosperous, classless and churchless future as incompatible with personal responsibility and autonomy. But more than the new government troubled him. The mission to Yugoslavia had revealed to him the willingness of Churchill's war-time coalition to betray its former allies among the resistance forces in favour of Moscow-backed partisans, and to hand over innocent refugees to persecution by Tito's Communists: it was not in 1940 only that 'the prisoners rolled away to slavery'. His report to the Foreign Office on this matter was ignored, so he wrote to *The Times* to condemn the Tito regime as having 'all the characteristics of Nazism' (*Essays*, p. 283). He was particularly attached to the Catholic culture of Hapsburg Europe, which he had come to admire when he visited Budapest for the Eucharistic Congress of 1938 (*Essays*, pp. 234–8), and he felt its betrayal deeply. In the Preface to the second edition (1947) of *Edmund Campion*, he wrote:

In fragments and whispers we get news of other saints in the prison camps of Eastern and South-eastern Europe, of cruelty and degradation more savage than anything in Tudor England, of the same, pure light shining in darkness, uncomprehended. (p. 8)

He sought consolation in the Faith. Clear-headed humanists, such as Arthur Koestler and George Orwell, apparently shared his disillusionment:

Nothing is in sight except a welter of lies, hatred, cruelty and ignorance . . . It is quite possible that man's major problems will *never* be solved. But it is also unthinkable! . . . So you get the quasi-mystical belief . . . that somehow, somewhere in space and time, human life will cease to be the miserable, brutish thing it now is. (George Orwell, *Collected Essays*, 1961, p. 231)

Reviewing this essay, Waugh wrote of Orwell:

He frequently brings his argument to the point when having, with great acuteness, seen the falsity and internal contradiction of the humanist view of life, there seems no alternative but the acceptance of revealed religion, and then stops short . . . I suspect he has never heard of Mgr Knox's *God and the Atom*, which begins where he ends and in an exquisitely balanced work of art offers what seems to me the only answer to the problem that vexes him. (*Essays*, pp. 306–7)

God and the Atom (1945) was written in horrified reaction to the dropping of atom bombs on Japan in 1945. It addresses the problem of how to sustain a God-centred view of the modern world. Religion was being challenged on two fronts, by the supposition that the chaotic and explosive nightmare of Relativity and Quantum Theory had finally disposed of the notion of an ordered universe, and by strategic thinking based on the principle that, war being 'a kind of all-in wrestling match', it was permissible to 'adopt every means to win it which opportunity [put] in your way' (p. 63), targeting civilians, dropping atom bombs, betraying your allies and innocent refugees who looked to you for protection. Both attitudes, Knox suggested, had dangerous implications, not so much for men's 'conscious motives . . . as [for] their mental background' (p. 76):

our imaginations are threatened with a break-down of hope, as they are threatened with a break-down of faith . . . we want to think clearly, and as calmly as the case allows, about the possibilities of disaster that lie before us. (p. 59)

'*God and the Atom* inspired me', Waugh wrote: 'It came at a time of deflation and blew into me a clear breath of reason and wisdom' (*Essays*, p. 350); it told him he had nothing to fear from 'the constitution of the Universe and the stream of History'.

Perhaps; but he could not achieve the clarity and calm which Knox prescribed. He rejoined his family. He travelled whenever he could, notably to Spain in 1946 and to Hollywood in 1947. His journalism was much in demand and he was well known for his idiosyncratic right-wing opinions. He adopted the manners of an irascible old man. His offensiveness to strangers was notorious, and some of his least tolerable behaviour was triumphantly recorded in his diary. He continued to take pleasure in his friends and his family. He and Laura had had four children by 1944 (one died) and were to have three more. But he seems to have been a difficult father, loving, demanding and intolerant. Even in his own home he was ill at ease with the world. 'The Church', he had written in 1938, 'teaches that man is by nature an exile' (*Essays*, p. 224) – we are, in the words of the ancient prayer, 'poor banished children of Eve'. That was fine in principle but hard to bear in practice. The author of works as vividly of their time as *Vile Bodies* and *Put Out More Flags* was finding it impossible to write about his own country and his present experience. He started an historical novel, based on the Empress Helena's supposed discovery of the wood of Christ's Cross, but progress was slow. He turned to short stories and the novelette. All of them register his estrangement from the world, and the presence in his mind of tensions and energies which neither Faith nor reason could quite control.

The short story was not suited to Waugh's talent. Except for the genial 'Cruise', the pre-war stories are hard-hearted pieces about loneliness, revenge, selfishness, cruelty, madness and death. The characters are types, and the text traps its readers into identifying with the losers or hating the winners. Alternatively we may share the author's glee by imagining others falling into the traps we have evaded. Waugh regarded these pieces as marketable experiments which might be incorporated into a later work. He was even prepared to re-cycle old metaphors. The children's game 'grandmother's steps', which describes Lady Marchmain's manipulative conversational tactics in *Brideshead Revisited* is used in *Helena* (1950) to suggest the guileless young heroine's shyness in conversation. Comparable transformations occur when whole incidents are transferred from short story to longer fictions: piquant snatches of narrative sadism are changed utterly in the setting of intellectual seriousness which informs even the lightest of Waugh's novels. (We have noted already this process in the incorporation of 'The Man Who Liked Dickens' into *A Handful of Dust* and the plundering of 'An Englishman's Home' for *Put Out More Flags*.) In the aftermath of the war, however, the awkward fragment, the savage conceit and the underdeveloped narrative were tossed at the public without apparent concern for wholeness and finish. These 'dissatisfying' narratives are, however, much more demanding than the pre-war short stories.

The first of Waugh's novelettes is *Scott-King's Modern Europe* (1947). The 'dim' Scott-King is set up as a portentous sign in an imperialist frame of reference. His classical scholarship is a cultural empire and a surrogate for Waugh's Catholicism. He sees the decline of his subject's popularity, and the rise of physics and economics as 'the victories of barbarism' (p. 198); when the war degenerates into 'a sweaty tug-of-war between teams of indistinguishable louts' (p. 199), he thinks of himself as an exile in his own country: 'he had wedded the Adriatic; he was a Mediterranean man' (p. 203). He is 'an adult, an intellectual, a classical scholar, almost a poet' (pp. 201–2). The sources of his dream are represented by the lovely town of Santa Maria – Athenian colony, Carthaginian port, Roman town, with a fine Dominican church, a piazza built by the Hapsburgs, a classical garden laid out by one of Napoleon's generals – 'Santa Maria', we are told – the name is not accidental – 'lay very near the heart of Europe' (p. 246).

The story (based partly on Waugh's Spanish journey) of how Scott-King is disabused of this dream has considerable comic and satirical potential, and the narrative of his journey to, and arrival in,

Neutralia suggests that the text is going to develop into a significant meditation on modernity. But the writing is sketchy, and the tone shifts unsettlingly. Promising ideas – the dim don who disgraces himself on the first night, the ace female reporter, the immensely tall Swedish sportswoman about whom Scott-King has Betjeman-style fantasies, the desperate expedients of Dr Fe to keep the Bellorious festival going, the sudden abandonment of Scott-King by his hosts – fail to compose themselves into a sustained run of frantic event or seriously orchestrated comedy. Intermittently the text even draws attention to its own limitations – 'You have heard all about Scott-King, but you have not met him' (p. 200) – 'To even the Comic Muse . . . there are forbidden places. Let us leave Scott-King then on the high seas' (p. 248). In fact 'the gadabout Muse' is blocked in *Scott-King's Modern Europe* by the rough intrusion into the text of current history in the person of Dr Bogdan Antonic, 'a middle-aged, gentle man whose face [is] lined with settled distress and weariness' (p. 220).

The choice of a Croat to represent the abandoned people of Eastern Europe is, of course, no accident. 'I am a Croat, born under the Hapsburg Empire,' Dr Antonic declares. '. . . As a young man I studied in Zagreb, Budapest, Prague, Vienna – one was free, one moved where one would; one was a citizen of Europe . . .' (ibid.) But the appalling thing about Waugh's narrative is that even Dr Antonic's story is left hanging like Miss Sveningen's Sports Congress – he and his family are people without a future. In their world, there is no possibility of a game even getting started; it would have been insulting to them, therefore, for Scott-King's to have solution. Only luck ensures that he doesn't end up a naked refugee in 'No 64 Jewish Illicit Immigrants' Camp, Palestine' (p. 248). Modern Europe is not a text in which any kind of meaning, no matter how provisional or farcical, can be generated.

But at least Scott-King is an engaging man, unlike the central character in other stories written around this time. With the publication of *Brideshead Revisited* Waugh had broken cover, and though he was never to write another first-person narrative, all his later fictions (except *Helena*) centre on a character whose experi-

ences and relationships apparently reflect his own. But in some of
the post-war stories, notably 'Tactical Exercise' (1947) and 'Love
Among the Ruins' (1953), his surrogate is mad or bad or dangerous
to identify with. It is as if he found some kind of release in identifying
with the nastier elements in minds like that of the elder Plant. The
hero of 'Tactical Exercise', for example, John Verney, is a mean-
spirited, anti-semitic ex-soldier, bent on murdering his wife, a civil
servant who is having an affair with a Jewish colleague:

> Elizabeth was part and parcel of it. She worked for the State and the Jews
> . . . And as the winter wore on . . . [she] grew in John Verney's despairing
> mind to more than human malevolence as the archpriestess and maenad of
> the century of the common man.
>   'You aren't looking well, John,' said his aunt. 'You and Elizabeth ought
> to get away for a bit. She is due for leave at Easter.'
>   'The State is granting her a supplementary ration of her husband's
> company, you mean . . .'
>   Uncle and aunt laughed uneasily . . . [John's] little jokes . . . sometimes
> struck chill in that family circle. Elizabeth regarded him gravely and silently.
> (pp. 165–6)

Elizabeth is intelligent, sympathetic and successful; John is a nasty
lunatic; yet Waugh deliberately pollutes some of his most honestly
felt convictions by passing them through John's mind. He then has
Elizabeth kill John off by the very means he had planned to murder
her. Could it be that John Verney represented something in Waugh
himself that he hated?

A similar sense of disorientation afflicts *Love Among the Ruins*
(1953). In this fantasy of the future, Britain is divided into two
classes, bureaucratic social workers and their miserable, pampered
clients. The only flourishing part of the state apparatus is the
Euthanasia Department, and Waugh happily consigns Parsnip and
Pimpernell to its tender mercies. His hero, Miles Plastic, the state-
reared orphan, is 'Modern Man', but his imprisonment for arson in
a beautiful country house (ironically called Mountjoy after the
hideous Dublin gaol) leaves him dissatisfied with a world dominated
by reproductions of Leger and Picasso, and a weekly diet of films.
The bearded ex-dancer Clara introduces him to love, to a lost
aestheticism in the form of two eighteenth-century paintings, and to

a sense of the relationship between them. She recalls how shocked her fellow-dancers were by the growth of her beard; she was the best in her class and can never work again.

'. . . What I try to explain [says Clara] is that it's just because I could dance that *I know* life is worth living . . . Does that sound very silly?'
    'It sounds unorthodox.'
    'Ah, but you are not an artist.' (p. 201)

In this fanciful reworking of Orwell's *1984*, however, Clara is Julia to Miles's Winston Smith, and betrays him by sacrificing their baby and her face to the sterile satisfactions of the dance. Miles, on the other hand, reverts happily to his incendiarism. In its way this is an exhilarating conclusion – until we recall the cries of the widows, mothers and orphans of the airmen he incinerated first time round.

The two most notable marks of this phase of Waugh's work are thus an unfinished quality in the story-telling and a central character whose solipsistic hatreds incite repugnance and invite approval. Both are evident in *The Loved One. An Anglo-American Tragedy* (1948), the outcome of the trip to Hollywood in 1947. It begins with a parody of stories of Empire by Kipling or Somerset Maugham, but the joke peters out. We have known all along that the setting is California, but the pretence might have been exploded with more panache. The note of parody persists, however. Dennis Barlow's professions – animal mortician and non-denominational clergyman – mark him out as the bounder in a Kipling or a Maugham story whose exclusion from colonial society is a test of either the man or the white community – but this too is underplayed. There is similarly unrealized potential in the professional quietus of Mr Slump, which fails to meet the standard set by Simon Balcairn in *Vile Bodies*. The comparison draws attention to the meanheartedness of Mr Slump's last piece of advice to a reader – 'Find a nice window and jump out' (p. 115): the world is no longer sweet enough for inventive farce.

    But in California such inventiveness was uncalled for. 'Whispering Glades' was fact. It was called Forest Lawns and Waugh wrote about it to his agent:

I am entirely obsessed by Forest Lawns . . . I go there two or three times a week, am on easy terms with the chief embalmer . . . It is wonderful literary material . . . I am at the heart of it. (*Letters*, p. 247)

With heavy irony, he reported Hollywood's 'Social life gay & refined'. Not Abyssinia nor Latin America, nor even modern Europe had prepared him for the guilelessness, insensitivity, money and religiosity of California, where Mexican temptresses were turned into Irish colleens, where there was no feeling for history or literature, where corpses were painted like whores, and where, though the graces of civilization were unknown, the prison-house of the mind was none the less kept firmly closed. Such a world was too barren for the shifts of sympathy and insight with which distant places had been treated in earlier novels. Aimée Thanatogenos (her name means the loved one of the people of death) is, admittedly, a Seth figure but her spirit has to be sought 'in the mountain air of the dawn, in the eagle-haunted passes of Hellas' (p. 105) and her eyes are 'greenish and remote, with a rich glint of lunacy' (p. 46). And she is alone. Mr Joyboy and Dr Kenworthy hardly fill the boots of the Earl of Ngumo and the Nestorian Patriarch, and if the English colony qualifies for the role of the Courtenays, Los Angeles could not provide acting room for General Connolly, Mr Youkoumian or Mr Baldwin, still less for Benito. Disconnection does not require diagnosis in *The Loved One*; it is served up with the setting as a matter of course, like the iced water.

What does require diagnosis is Dennis Barlow. Superficially he is an urbane figure with whom the reader can identify, mildly victimized as the hero of a comic narrative ought to be, the appraiser of absurdities in a strange land, like Gulliver in the Third Part of *Gulliver's Travels*, who comes out on top by luck and guile. Actually he is a monster, the embodiment of the daemonic element in Waugh's work. His relationship with Aimée is a partial replay of Basil Seal's with Prudence. We go along with the joke of Dennis and Mr Joyboy's rivalry for Aimée's heart, and rejoice at the inventiveness of Dennis's plagiarisms and the prospect of their discovery, but his insensitivity towards Aimée generates unease. With an economy matching the treatment of Prudence in a similar situation, Waugh transforms Aimée in their last encounter into a person one has met and may any moment meet again, and the effect on Dennis's standing is unsettling. As he blathers on about his new vestments, she turns on him and says, in the honest accents of ordinary life, 'Oh, do be quiet! You bore me so' (p. 110). We enjoy his cleverness when he talks about the psychological affinity between them but there is something approaching coarseness in his refusal to release her from her vow. It is no surprise when he incinerates her without a pang and for a consideration.

But Dennis is no Basil. As an artist and author's front man, he is in touch with his feelings. He is a dissident; his mind encloses the graces of civilization and the energies of the savage:

Dennis listened intently . . . Whispering Glades held him in thrall. In that zone of insecurity in the mind where none but the artist dare trespass, the tribes were mustering. Dennis, the frontiersman, could read the signs. (p. 64)

It is on this note that the story ends:

On the last evening in Los Angeles Dennis knew he was a favourite of Fortune . . . He was leaving . . . not only unravished but enriched. He was adding his bit to the wreckage, something that had long irked him, his young heart, and was carrying back instead the artist's load, a great, shapeless chunk of experience . . . to work on it hard and long, for God knew how long. For that moment of vision a lifetime is often too short. (p. 127)

The Loved One is thus a serious attempt to develop ideas which first appeared in Waugh's work when John Plant identified himself with Humboldt's Gibbon and Charles Ryder described the secret which artists never share with ordinary people. But whereas Charles's art is betrayed by ingratiating conventionality (the 'charm' condemned by Anthony Blanche), Dennis's atavistic glee is as uningratiating as John Verney's malice or Miles Plastic's incendiarism. In Love Among the Ruins Clara declares, perhaps complacently, that being able to dance has taught her that life is worth living – in the end, after all, she prefers the dance to life and thereby betrays her art. Miles, on the other hand, becomes the true artist when, in the final paragraph, his cigarette lighter produces 'a tiny flame – gemlike, hymeneal, auspicious'. This aligns Miles with Walter Pater's celebrated assertion that for the true devotee of art success in life is to 'burn always with [a] hard, gemlike flame, to maintain his ecstasy' (*The Renaissance. Studies in Art and Poetry*, 1961 ed., p. 222). This is a remarkable allusion. Pater stands for a relativized view of identity in a deterministic universe where the spirit struggles to maintain the mere illusion of freedom. He explicitly denies stability to what Waugh called 'a writer's material . . . the preconception of Christendom', namely the individual soul (*Essays*, p. 206). Yet Waugh takes Paterian aestheticism even further into the territory of radical doubt than Pater would have thought proper. He compels art and Christianity, from their different points of view, to confront the exhilarating provocations and promises of madness and death, or, as Georges Bataille, the French critic and pornographer, expressed it, of 'Evil'.

If Waugh had glanced at Bataille's *Literature and Evil* he would have dismissed it as bosh. Had he read it he would have denounced it as wicked bosh. Nevertheless Bataille's ideas suggest why literature is spayed and homogenized in Whispering Glades. 'Good' in Bataille's terminology is rational and prudential; it aims, in Knox's words, 'to think clearly and calmly', to preserve life; it belongs to what Bataille calls 'the prosaic world of activity – where objects which are clearly extrinsic to the subject have a fundamental sense of the future' (Georges Bataille, *Literature and Evil*, 1973, p. 28). It opposes itself to sickness and death: 'The mainspring of human activity', Bataille maintains, 'is generally to reach the point furthest from the funereal domain, which is rotten, dirty and impure' (p. 48). In these terms California and Whispering Glades witness to 'the good society'. But in that case they are also confined to what Bataille calls 'feeble communication' (p. 171), yet feeble communication, he argues, is only possible because 'powerful communication' underlies it, and powerful communication demands 'an acute form of Evil' (p. ix). Powerful communication is therefore 'primary':

The habitual activity of beings . . . separates them from the privileged moments of powerful communication which is based on the emotions of sensuality, festivity, drama, love, separation and death. (pp. 171–2)

And childishness also – 'that arbitrary element born of the violence and puerile instincts of the past' (p. 7).

It is in this puerile, erotic, death-relishing spirit that Dennis lives for us, restoring our sense of the ecstatic and barbaric, which is the precondition of feeble communication and yet threatens both it and the future orientated world which feeble communication constructs. *The Loved One* accordingly fulfils the task of literature by generating in its readers a sense of exhilarating anxiety. Hence our enjoyment of Dennis's habit of keeping his supper in the refrigerator along with the animal cadavers, and his thoughts about the hanged Sir Francis:

'I think I understand. Well, let me assure you Sir Francis was quite white.'
    As he said this there came vividly into Dennis's mind the image which lurked there, seldom out of sight for long; the sack of body suspended and the face above it with eyes red and horribly starting from their sockets, the cheeks mottled in indigo like the marbled end-papers of a ledger and the tongue swollen and protruding like an end of black sausage. (p. 39)

This is prose making a festival of death's rottenness and impurity. Such themes, Bataille suggests,

constitute the basis of true literary emotion. Death alone . . . introduces that break without which nothing reaches . . . ecstasy . . . we thereby regain . . . both innocence and intoxication. (p. 13)

Bataille's argument is a proto-deconstructionist one. His law-governed world of feeble communication is provisional and unstable, and that which underlies it, a ludic, orgiastic, disgusting surrender to powerful communication, is a mystical state of 'sovereignty' in which the 'isolated being *loses himself*, in something . . . [so] unlimited . . . it is not even a thing: it is *nothing*' (p. 65). This ground of our being can even be denominated 'God'. 'There is nothing in religion,' Bataille writes, 'which cannot be found in poetry' (ibid.). But Catholicism, as Knox represents it, is built on feeble communication, on the establishment – in Bataille's words – of 'humble truths which coordinate our attitudes and activity with those of our fellow human beings' (p. 170), on thinking clearly, and as calmly as the case allows. To claim that communication 'is never stronger than when communication, in [this] weak sense . . . fails and becomes the equivalent of darkness' is to opt for what Waugh dismissed as mumbo-jumbo. Yet this is what Waugh himself seems to be doing when he celebrates 'that zone of insecurity in the mind where none but the artist dare trespass'. Could it be that Old-meadow was right after all, and that Waugh's Catholicism and his art really are at loggerheads?

Helena might have been written with the intention of suppressing precisely these doubts. Evil, as Bataille understands it, abounds in the novel; evil which Dennis Barlow would have stored away for future use, but which Helena contemptuously dismisses:

Helena had prayed, year by year, devoutly and at ease at the altars of her household and her people, had greeted the returning Spring with sacrifices, had sought to placate the powers of death, had honoured the sun and the earth and the fertile seed. But the religious ladies of Ratisbon spoke of secret meetings, passwords, initiations, trances, and extraordinary sensations . . . of enigmatic voices, of standing stark naked in a pit while a bull bled to death on the lattice above them.
   'It's all bosh, isn't it,' she said to the Governor's wife.
   'It's disgusting.'
   'Yes, but it's bosh, too, isn't it?' (pp. 42–3)

This is what makes her a suitable partner for Constantius who has a 'simple, earthly task' (p. 66) to perform, and a vision to sustain him in his pursuit of it:

   'I'm not a sentimental man,' said Constantius, 'but I love the wall. Think of it . . . inside, peace, decency, the law, the altars of the Gods, industry, the arts, order; outside, wild beasts and savages, forest and swamp, bloody mumbo-jumbo, men like wolf-packs . . .' (p. 39)

In the interest of this vision he foregoes advancement into the higher mysteries of Mithraism. Not so Constantine and Fausta, the devotees of witchcraft, or *Malefice*, which for Bataille is the profoundest engagement with Evil open to human beings. *Sacrifice*, he argues (such as Helena's people engage in), softens Evil by associating death 'with the purest, holiest . . . most conservative cares . . . the maintenance of life and work . . . [but] Malefice . . . [is] carried out for alien ends, often opposed to Good' (p. 52). This is consistent with Fausta's young black witch stepping 'off the causeway of time and place into trackless swamp' (p. 116) – and into a nightmare of a hideously recognizable twentieth-century Evil: '*Zivio! Viva! Arriba! Heil!*' The implications seem clear: whatever the excitements of *The Loved One*, *Helena* offers a vision of common sense trying first to associate itself with the earthly City, then being caught up into the City of God and the glory of sanctity and miracle, while remaining in unaffected contact with humble truths which coordinate our attitudes and activity with those of our fellow human beings.

What has to be decided in relation to *Helena*, however, is not the nature of the project but the adequacy of Waugh's approach to history. It is true that Jewish and Christian history has always been read as both fact and sign; any narrative can be a type of the truth. Waugh's apparently blasphemous parallel between Aphrodite summoning Helen of Troy to the bed of Paris and the Holy Spirit summoning Helena to the scene of Christ's Passion is thus legitimate. But he infuses his symbolism with an unsettling facetiousness. On the one hand we are in a fantasy world: Helena is the daughter of 'Old King Cole' (fiddlers three in attendance); the Wandering Jew tells her the location of the Cross in a dream; and she ends her days as a kind of fairy godmother. On the other, her world is amusingly familiar: Army wives in Treves chatter like Army wives in Gibraltar. The lower degrees of Mithraism are redolent of Freemasonry with Mithraic priests keeping a crafty eye on their rich and powerful initiates – for priests of all religions are the same. The text is well stocked with amusing anachronisms – references to 'Government House' and 'the Balkans'. King Coel as bluff English gentleman not Celtic Chieftain, Helena as a horse-mad adolescent. The result is a witty narrative which often makes a confusingly reductive impression.

The following exchange between Helena and Coel is typical:

'I must go with Constantius, papa, wherever he goes. Besides, he's
promised to take me to The City.'
  'The City indeed! . . . *Awful* place . . . You'll never get there . . . You'll be
stuck all your life in some Balkan barracks, you see.'
  'I must go with Constantius. After all, papa, we Trojans are always in
exile, aren't we – poor banished children of Teucer?' (p. 31)

At one level this appears to explicate the mythical; the legend that
the Britons were descended from Trojan exiles expresses a truth: the
entire human race is in exile. Equally it appears to make 'human
nature' as permanent as conservative theory requires – history is
after all an endless recycling of the same old problems. But the
anachronisms also remind us that the text is a modern construct,
and that if it validates anything it only does so tendentiously. Both
Coel and Helena are right – Constantius will keep her in the
Balkans, but their son will bring her first to Rome, then to Jerusalem
– yet there is nothing wonderful in that since the entire conversation
has been set up with precisely those ends in view.
  It is hard to see how such writing can escape its own lightness.
Where, for example, does Waugh's facetiousness leave Macarius
who seems to share Helena's sense of the importance and uncon-
tentiousness of 'fact', and who, like the Empress and Pope Sylvester,
is listed among the Catholic Saints?

Macarius reminded [Constantine] of the glories of Zion . . . Was it then
perhaps that [Constantine's] shadowy mind saw in a first reflected gleam the
opposed faces of history and myth? . . . had Constantine ever made a
distinction between the stories that were told of Galilee and those of
Olympus? Now for the first time he was talking face to face with a man who
handled . . . the identical wreath of thorn which had crowned the dying God
three hundred years ago.
  'Can you be sure?'
  'But of course, sir. Ever since that day the Church of Jerusalem has
guarded it . . .' (pp. 131–2)

There is of course no 'of course' about it, since Waugh's witty verbal
game-playing has subverted the status of fact. That Macarius's
speech nevertheless expresses what the novel is about is strongly
suggested by an article Waugh wrote on St Helena which argues that
her life's work discloses the essence of the Christian claim –

the unreasonable assertion that God became man and died on the Cross; not a myth or an allegory; true God, truly incarnate, tortured to death at a particular moment in time, at a particular geographical place, as a matter of plain historical fact. (*Essays*, p. 410)

The doctrine of the Incarnation which Waugh is affirming here may be summed up as the doctrine of God's involvement in the world of feeble communication, of humble truth: but all Waugh seems to make of it in the novel is to use Helena's history to illustrate yet again the notion that in the household of the Faith natural and supernatural grace rub along together famously. It is therefore difficult to see how stories told of Galilee can be clearly distinguished from those told of Olympus. It is hardly surprising that some reviewers felt that, as one of them put it, Waugh had left 'the heart of the matter to others and [concentrated] on the trimmings instead' (*Evelyn Waugh: The Critical Heritage*, 1984, p. 320). In then describing the book as 'amusing, shapely and well-written' (p. 321), this critic implied that Waugh was more interested in charming his readers than in convincing them, in effect, that *Helena* is at heart an anti-intellectual novel: ' "Oh *books*," said Helena' (p. 76). This theme is more grandly adumbrated in the potentially reductive conclusion to Helena's prayer to the Magi:

'You are . . . patrons . . . of all who have a tedious journey to make to the truth, of all who are confused with knowledge and speculation, of all who through politeness make themselves partners in guilt, of all who stand in danger by reason of their talents . . .

'For His sake who did not reject your curious gifts, pray always for all the learned, the oblique, the delicate. Let them not be quite forgotten at the Throne of God when the simple come into their kingdom.' (p. 145)

Intellectual integrity is often in danger when 'the simple' are aggrandized in this fashion.

On closer examination, however, the attack on discourse in *Helena* turns out to be cogent as well as deeply felt. (Helena's prayer to the Magi recalls an entry in Waugh's diary for 6 January 1945, in which the Epiphany is described as 'the feast of artists' and the Magi as clumsy intellectuals brought to Bethlehem by 'book-learning and speculation' (*Diaries*, p. 606). For the problem of intellectual activity extends beyond the representation of heretics as pedlars of esoteric nonsense, and proleptically the author of *The Decline and Fall of the Roman Empire* as a gibbon dying prematurely in the chill river mist. Lactantius makes a serious point when he says that a skilful historian (like Gibbon) might one day misrepresent the Christianization of the Empire: he 'might be refuted again and again but what he wrote would remain in people's minds when the refutations were quite forgotten' (p. 80). Lactantius also reaches the remarkable conclusion that words can '*do anything except generate their own meaning*' (p. 79) (my emphasis). This directly contradicts the current critical orthodoxy that words are like cards in Mrs Rattery's game of Patience, their meaning being generated exclusively by the system of rules governing their use, rather than by the accuracy with which they make reference to the real world. But in proposing through Lactantius a conservative rebuttal of such theories of meaning, Waugh puts his own literary values at risk, for Lactantius (whom Gibbon dismissed as an eloquent but naïve propagandist) is a writer after Waugh's own heart – delighting 'in the joinery and embellishment of his sentences' (p. 79) – yet it is his skills which are dismissed as 'the kitten games of syntax and rhetoric'. Waugh's distrust of language has deepened. He began by ridiculing journalese in *Scoop*. He then discovered, in the reminiscences of John Plant and Charles Ryder, the self-betraying character of style. Now craftmanship itself is seen as potentially deceptive. One reason, therefore, why *Helena* is so frivolous may be that Waugh actually wishes to foreground the triviality of the kitten game on which he is engaged. He is not only claiming that to distinguish bosh from the truth one must identify the reality to which truthful words refer; he is also acknowledging that this is not a simple matter for any writer – for the poor agnostic Gibbon, for the conservative theorist, for the orthodox theologian, or for the skilful novelist. All writing is at a remove from reality, yet loses touch with it at its peril.

Theology, therefore, even the solemn teaching of the Council of Nicaea, gets short shrift in *Helena*. Politics also. The problem with Constantius's vision of imperialist order is that in its devotion to *Realpolitik*, it is indifferent to the possibility of mystery and to notions of justice. The 'grim story' (p. 47) of Tetricus's betrayal of his army and its slaughter by Constantius, is disturbing not only as an atrocity (so reminiscent of the betrayals of Croats and White Russians by Western Governments in 1945) but as evidence of the moral myopia of the worldly: Constantius cannot see the implications of his story. In the context of such horrors one can understand what motivates the draper who outdistances him in the race for Mithraic enlightenment: as Knox notes in *God and the Atom*, even Christians can be disconcerted by a world in which wickedness flourishes. But the integrated nature, he suggests, does not seek relief by flight. Rather it

finds a unity in all things; even what is bad . . . points it, somehow, to the contemplation of the good that has been betrayed, the higher good that has been missed. And in that contemplation it rests undisturbed. (p. 142)

The 'reality' which gives meaning to the kitten game of fiction in *Helena* – the heart of the matter – is just such an integrated nature. What we can rely on is not historical, not even the wood of the cross – the novel makes clear what Waugh states explicitly in his article on St Helena, that Helena may have been mistaken about that – but the character of the individual soul that 'invented' it:

She had done what only the saints succeed in doing; what indeed constitutes their patent of sanctity. She had completely conformed to the will of God. Others a few years back had done their duty gloriously in the arena. Hers was a gentler task, merely to gather wood. (p. 156)

The scope and the limitations of this affirmation are significant. It confirms Waugh's recognition that the system of differences on which his own world was constructed was flimsy and provisional. The Kingdom belongs to 'the simple'. Helena's intuitive vision of the Universal Church, of The City breaking out from behind the wall and covering the earth, is as subversive of Waugh's notions of class as it is of Constantius's imperialism. Both depend on distinctions that cannot be sustained under the Christian dispensation:

The intimate family circle of which she was a member bore no mark of kinship. The barrow-man grilling his garlic sausages in the gutter, the fuller behind his reeking public pots, the lawyer or the lawyer's clerk, might each and all be one with the Empress Dowager in the Mystical Body. And the abounding heathen might in any hour become one with them. (p. 93)

More significantly, the Church's inclusiveness extends to the moral sphere. Thus Pope Sylvester remarks on the mixed nature of the Church's membership:

'. . . We look back already to the time of the persecution as though it were the heroic age, but have you ever thought how awfully few martyrs there were, compared with how many there ought to have been? The Church isn't a cult for a few heroes. It is the whole of fallen mankind redeemed. And of course just at the moment we're getting a lot of rather shady characters rolling in, just to be on the winning side.' (p. 127)

Including, of course, Constantine himself, whom Waugh represents as murderous, mad and evil. He, too, is finally baptized. There is no limit to the power of Grace; it can obliterate even the distinction between the 'sovereignty' of Evil and the sovereignty of God.

However, in thus identifying a disposition of the will in an individual human soul as the essential condition for an integrated and integrating relationship with Fact, and illustrating it in the person of a saint, Waugh does no more than establish his case in principle; for even if we find Helena's personality convincing, the novel still leaves unaddressed the two great problems haunting all Waugh's work after 1945 – the problem of Evil in the human heart and the problem of exile in the modern world. The struggle between Knox and the daemon for mastery over Waugh's writing was still unresolved.

The Loved One and Helena were reassuring to Waugh. The former was a runaway commercial success and was respected in literary circles – he was at pains to publish it first in Cyril Connolly's Horizon. The latter was his most thoughtful book to date; it was a happy performance articulating his sense of the coherence of his Faith. He thus had excellent grounds for believing that his powers as an artist, daemonic and technical, and his Christian humanist vision of European civilization, had survived the rough intrusion of modern history into his life and imagination. He had also recovered something of his old spirit. His letters to his friends at this time were often masterly – the correspondence with Nancy Mitford and Ann Fleming in particular is always worth re-reading. He was an uncalculating letter-writer, intemperate, a gossip, but on occasion vulnerable. He often gave offence, but he was capable of generous contrition, and was rarely dull.

His journalism was equally engaging. He wrote energetically about artists he admired – Chaplin, Wodehouse, Compton-Burnett, Hemingway – and on Catholic subjects dear to his heart: his essays on American Catholicism, the Holy Land, and the shrine of St Francis Xavier in Goa (he had a special affection for Jesuits and Goans) reveal a confident sense of history and of the Church as the chief work of God within it. And by the Church Waugh meant all Helena's fellow-worshippers. A passage about 'the heroic fidelity of Negro Catholics' in 'The American Epoch in the Catholic Church' reads:

The Church has not always been a kind mother to them. Everywhere in the South Catholic planters brought their slaves to the sacraments, but in the bitter years after the Reconstruction few whites, priests or laity, recognized any special obligation towards them. Often they could only practice their religion at the cost of much humiliation. Some drifted from the Church to preposterous sects or reverted to paganism, but many families remained steadfast. Theirs was a sharper test than the white Catholics had earlier undergone, for here the persecutors were fellow-members in the Household of the Faith. But, supernaturally, they knew the character of the Church better than their clergy. (*Essays*, p. 383)

He wrote with unaffected admiration about Thomas Merton, the American Cistercian; Edith Stein, the Jewish philosopher, Carmelite nun and victim of the Nazis – her conversion impressed Waugh because it was 'so cool and impersonal' (*Essays*, p. 434) yet led to 'a new life of devotion and prayer' – and Pope John XXIII, whose election to the papacy at the age of 77 evoked for him the twin Mysteries of Providence and Vocation.

But in other respects he was not happy. By 1950, he was earning less than his manner of life and large family required. He was restless. Having considered moving to Ireland, he finally decided to move to another substantial country house in Gloucestershire. His work was frequently reviewed offensively. Even a sympathetic reviewer accused him of depicting 'Mother Church as one Big Dorm and her mysteries as so much sacred larking' (*Critical Heritage*, p. 339); Kingsley Amis suggested he might be turning 'into a kind of storm-trooper' (*Critical Heritage*, p. 371) from the sixth form of a Catholic public school; and Donat O'Donnell (Conor Cruise O'Brien) wrote of 'his almost idolatrous reverence for birth and wealth' (*Critical Heritage*, p. 258) and argued that his religion was tainted by 'nostalgia for childhood, snobbery, neo-Jacobitism' (p. 259). He suffered excruciating bouts of boredom and irascibility. He was drinking and eating heavily and dosing himself with sleeping drugs. But he still needed an audience to arrange his thoughts for. His reaction, though fuelled by rage and panic, was full of guile. He roundly declared he had done with the world, dressed in beautifully tailored suits of loud check, barricaded himself in his country home, and defied all comers to disturb his peace.

The world responded by treating him as a monster and a joke, and not always judiciously – he won two libel actions against Express Newspaper journalists. Another of his well-publicized vendettas was with the Oxford historian Hugh Trevor-Roper (Lord Dacre) who made a careless but obstinately defended reference to St John Fisher and St Thomas More. Waugh in the end advised him to 'change his name and seek a livelihood at Cambridge' (*Letters*, p. 644), advice the historian subsequently followed. On religious matters Waugh could be mischievously provocative. He expressed regret at the failure of the Spanish Armada, (*Essays*, p. 467), and claimed that he would like to see some 'progressive' Catholics incinerated at an *auto-da-fé* (*Essays*, p. 490). His political alienation was encapsulated in a notorious justification for never having voted in a parliamentary election – 'I do not aspire to advise my sovereign in her choice of servants' (*Essays*, p. 537), a declaration which combines an acute insight into the hypocrisies of the British constitution with epigrammatic pith and urbane self-parody.

All this was effective enough in ensuring that he enjoyed his privacy without losing his audience, but it was not the behaviour of a comfortable man. Nevertheless he kept on writing. In 1952, he published *Men at Arms*, the first of a projected trilogy – a serious war book, if not the one he had planned in 1935 – but he was dissatisfied with it. Then early in 1954, hoping to make progress with the second volume, he went on a winter cruise to Ceylon. He was drinking heavily and dosing himself on chloral. While on board ship, he began to hear radio programmes about himself from the pipes in his cabin, then the voices of a team of psychologists. To his surprise these experiences continued when he quitted the ship and flew on to his destination. He wrote to Laura about them. She cabled him to return home by air, which he did. When she 'pointed out inconsistencies in his delusions, he accepted them and saw first Father Caraman [S.J.] and then E. B. Strauss, a Roman Catholic psychoanalyst. Chloral was banned and paraheldehyde substituted. [He] recovered immediately' (*Letters*, p. 421). Within two weeks of his final deluded letter from Ceylon, he was giving an account of his 'sharp but brief attack of insanity' to Nancy Mitford. By October he was well into the second novel in the trilogy, *Officers and Gentlemen* (1955), which he finished. But he felt the project had run out of steam, and announced its termination. He had been thinking clearly, however, and as calmly as the case allowed, about his madness. The result was *The Ordeal of Gilbert Pinfold. A Conversation Piece*.

At one level *The Ordeal of Gilbert Pinfold* is virtually plotless. Mr Pinfold, fifty-year-old author, Catholic convert and family man, goes on a cruise for the sake of his health and to get on with a book. He drinks too much, takes sleeping drugs and has hallucinations; like Gulliver returning from the land of the Houyhnhnms, he cannot gauge the effect of his behaviour on his fellow-passengers. He sends alarming letters to his wife and she cables him to return home; he does so, defies his voices and, unlike Gulliver, takes his wife into his confidence; she persuades him to see their doctor, who puts it all down to the drug-taking – but he rejects this simple-minded diagnosis: 'he had endured a great ordeal, and unaided, had emerged the victor' (p. 156); so he sets to work to write a story called *The Ordeal of Gilbert Pinfold*.

This simple recursive structure is, however, the basis for a minutely plotted narrative. The victim of delusions like Mr Pinfold's is constrained to reason 'closely about his situation' (p. 51), that is to generate increasingly complicated and unlikely explanations both for the failure of his delusions to accord with reality, and for the reactions they provoke in others. The stress generated by such efforts is generally so exhausting that few patients afflicted in this way are critical of the solutions which their imaginations come up with. Mr Pinfold, however, remains an alert critic of the unfolding drama in his head, the expert audience for whom his own deluded thoughts are being arranged. At the same time, of course, he is their author, the source of the drama's inspirations, the craftsman who gives them shape and meaning. The madder he becomes, therefore, the greater the demands upon his authorial powers. His delusions stretch his abilities both as a critic and as a writer of fiction to the utmost; he has a professional as well as a psychological stake in the skill with which he fends off the rough intrusion of sanity into his consciousness.

The narrative is consequently a sustained essay in suspense. How will Mr Pinfold's fantasies get themselves out of the impossible situations they have got themselves into? Alone in his cabin in the middle of the night, and convinced he is to be handed over to a Spanish boarding party, he bursts into the corridor to offer himself for the sacrifice not as a dupe but as 'a garlanded hero' (p. 97) – like Lady Marchmain's brothers – only to find the *Caliban* silent and in perfect order:

> He had been dauntless a minute before in the face of his enemies. Now he was struck with real fear . . . possessed from outside himself with atavistic panic. 'O let me not be mad, not mad, sweet heaven,' he cried. (p. 98)

But Lear's words save him. They remind him of the sadistic woman whom he has named 'Goneril'. He has only to hear her laugh and the entire 'Spanish' episode is explained: it was all a trick to humiliate him: 'he might be ridiculous; but he was not mad'. One of Freud's dreamers could not have had a more economical set of associations.

Equally resourceful is the resolution of the defloration episode. Again Mr Pinfold is a quixotic figure, roused this time to a state of undignified sexual expectation at the prospect of a devoted virgin eager to learn from him the art of love; but of course 'Margaret' cannot materialize. Again he leaves his cabin; again the corridor is empty, though he can hear the voices of his 'persecutors' and the snores of a fellow-passenger. It is crucial for his credit as 'author' and 'audience' that the device of the hoax should not be repeated, so he gets cross and returns to his bunk to await 'Margaret's' arrival. Then he hears her weeping. She thinks the other passenger's snores are Mr Pinfold's and that he has rejected her.

> The last voice Mr Pinfold heard before he fell asleep was Goneril's: 'Snoring? Shamming. Gilbert knew he wasn't up to it. He's impotent, aren't you, Gilbert? Aren't you?'
> 'It was Glover snoring,' said Mr Pinfold, but nobody seemed to hear him. (p. 119)

He thus ruefully enters into the undignified subject-position his plot has created for himself, but his sexual *amour propre* is a small price to pay for the salvation of his meaning.

That meaning is a thoroughly literary construct. When he 'discovers' that his voices have been controlled by Angel, the BBC interviewer, he feels 'as though he had come to the end of an ingenious, old-fashioned detective novel which he had read rather inattentively' (p. 127). Actually the world he makes for himself is more like a parodic mixture of late Victorian boys' stories — ' "By God, I'll shoot the first man of you that moves," said the officer' (p. 47) — and imperialist thrillers of the school of John Buchan. Mr Pinfold's nightmare is that, as in Buchan's fiction, apparently archetypal Britishers, in this case the ship's master and 'the General', may well be villains in disguise, while his own credentials as an English gentleman are called in question. He is condemned as a Jew, a homosexual, a social climber, a coward, a communist and a snob. But this conventionalized nightmare of prejudice and stereotyping has explanatory power. It functions in his ordeal as 'ideology' is said to function in society, as an illusion of connectedness concealing contradiction.

Mr Pinfold, of course, would have been unimpressed by the claims of materialists that our perceptions of the world all have this illusory character. The sane part of him, at least, judges itself to be unproblematically in touch with the world of fact; he *knows* where he is.

> The sea might have been any sea by the look of it, but he knew it was the Mediterranean, that splendid enclosure which held all the world's history and half the happiest memories of his own life; of work and rest and battle, of aesthetic adventure, and of young love. (p. 100)

This suggests that his essential identity is finally wedded to an ability to distinguish between a deluded, morally reductive world of 'Northern European' imperialist fantasy, and that other world, classical and Catholic, in which his true self lives and moves and has its being. But the delusions of a madman, like a deliberately fantastical narrative such as *Helena*, can only signify indirectly the providentially ordered historical frame in which real lives are lived. The heart of the matter in both texts, therefore, the reality which each must succeed in referring to, is the *will* of its central character. That is why Mr Pinfold's identification of existentialism and psychoanalysis as twin evils in contemporary culture is intellectually entirely serious. Everything may depend on his defying the voices' suggestion that he should tell his wife that he is cured, but we are concerned with much more than a single decision. Even when deluded, Mr Pinfold has continuous responsibility for his choices, and just as Helena must be seen to live a life that taken as a whole seems convincingly to conform to the will of God, so Mr Pinfold must seem to be capable of deciding for himself even when he is off his head.

The two aspects of the text which serve this project best are the modesty of its claims on Mr Pinfold's behalf and its recursiveness. The note of modesty appears in the opening account of Mr Pinfold as a writer and a Catholic. The man, whom his non-Catholic critics regard as 'bigoted rather than pious' (p. 13), is in fact a figure of fun:

> at the very time when the leaders of his Church were exhorting their people to emerge from the catacombs into the forum, to make their influence felt in democratic politics and to regard worship as a corporate rather than a private act, Mr Pinfold burrowed ever deeper into the rock. Away from his

parish he sought the least frequented Mass; at home he held aloof from the multifarious organizations which have sprung into being at the summons of the hierarchy to redeem the times.

The historical allusions here – catacombs, forum, rock – are precise and combined with an authentically ecclesial vocabulary – 'corporate . . . act', 'redeem the times' – make the bishops' call and Mr Pinfold's resolute refusal to answer it both serious and funny at the same time. As his adventures unfold, he pursues his goals with a nice mixture of simplicity and worldliness. At the beginning of the 'Spanish' crisis he thinks 'of Jenkins's ear and the Private of the Buffs' (p. 85) – the literacy of the references contrasting well with the naïvety of the sentiment. Nor are we surprised to read how this worldly, intellectual madman 'composed himself for sleep' (p. 112) in obedience to the injunctions of the Penny Catechism. Most finely judged of all is his account of his ordeal when it is over – it was 'exciting' (p. 154) – he is 'like a warrior returned from a hard fought victory' (pp. 154–5) – but he is also his old, self-knowing self. 'It was very brave of you to turn down the offer', says Mrs Pinfold of the pact of silence proposed to him by the voices. ' "It was sheer bad temper," [says] Mr Pinfold quite truthfully.' (p. 155) This is a 'Catholic' mentality trying, rationally and deliberately, to conform to God's will, in madness and out of it.

The loop-back conclusion is Mr Pinfold's own most emphatic statement about this autonomy. By returning to its starting-point, the narrative confronts the fact that Mr Pinfold's claim to be the outcome of his own free and responsible decisions is itself recursive: it must be self-justifying or nothing:

He was neither a scholar nor a regular soldier; the part for which he cast himself was a combination of eccentric don and testy colonel and he acted it strenuously, before his children at Lychpole and his cronies in London, until it came to dominate his whole outward personality. When he ceased to be alone, when he swung into his club or stumped up the nursery stairs, he left half of himself behind, and the other half swelled to fill its place. He offered the world a front of pomposity mitigated by indiscretion, that was as hard, bright, and antiquated as a cuirass. (p. 15)

It is only when we re-read this passage as Mr Pinfold's own that we can see the questions it raises. Was Mr Pinfold 'alone' – in other words, a complete self, not a self-selected persona – when he wrote these words, or is the entire text a continuation of his scholar-soldier act, or some other pose, say that of a guilefully self-describing author? But of course such questions are unanswerable. What we are invited to 'see' is that the self-constructions, self-bifurcations, self-disclosures and, above all, the knowingness of the text about its own paradoxes, do not set up a vicious regress but constitute a style, a fist, a way of willing which is one with a way of telling, and which justifies Mr Pinfold's confidence that he can maintain his essential identity to the scrap heap.

Mr Pinfold, then, is no W. H. Henley. He is bloody but unbowed, the master of his fate, the captain of his soul, but he also expects his readers to catch him in the act of calculating their reactions to his saying so. Or so we may speculate, for Mr Pinfold is only a character we construct as we read a text of which he is not the author. It would have been impossible, after all, for a writer as literate as he to ignore the fact that the ship and its master in his text bear the names of two celebrated literary characters. Unless, of course, he is using this device to signal that all names in the text have been changed, including his own.

In that case may we read 'Mr Pinfold' as 'Evelyn Waugh'? By Waugh's own admission, after all, the novel draws upon his actual monodrama on the high seas. But we need also to remember that the audience for whom these thoughts were being arranged included (among others) the *Daily Express* and its readers on the one hand, and the liberal intelligentsia – Kingsley Amis, Hugh Trevor-Roper and the implacable Conor Cruise O'Brien – on the other. Would Waugh have set himself up as a sitting shot for such a readership? Reviewing the novel for the *Spectator*, O'Brien, for example, suggested that Waugh excelled in 'the comic treatment of the grimmest themes . . . but not when he is treating sacred subjects, such as himself' (*Critical Heritage*, p. 381). The egregious offensiveness of this judgement, however, was precisely what both Evelyn Waugh and Gilbert Pinfold had come to expect from their critics. It was indeed part of the novel's meaning, or at any rate a precondition of that meaning, even before a word of O'Brien's review had been typed. In other words, Waugh needed the outraged critic as a stand-up comic needs a fall-guy: O'Brien simply leapt out of the audience, eager to play his destined role and give the text a significance it might otherwise have lacked. Words, after all, can do anything except generate their own meaning, and without the jeering of Waugh's critics the novel would have been trapped in the incipient solipsism of its recursiveness. Read as a study in self-portraiture before a largely uncomprehending and partially hostile audience, however, its anchorage in its own times becomes apparent, and it is revealed as a comic treatment of great sophistication and seriousness.

The first chapter is remarkable for its combination of frankness and vivid phrasing:

he looked at the world *sub specie aeternitatis* and he found it flat as a map; except when, rather often, personal annoyance intruded. Then he would come tumbling from his exalted point of observation. Shocked by a bad bottle of wine, an impertinent stanger, or a fault in syntax, his mind like a cinema camera trucked furiously forward to confront the offending object close-up with a glaring lens. (pp. 4–5)

A simple simile concealing a philosophically sophisticated concept leads first to an admission of petty fastidiousness (the man who thinks in terms of eternity makes a fuss about bad wine, bad manners and bad writing), then to the great comic image of the glaring cine-camera lens. For this is not just a description of a character – it is Waugh himself to the life, pinning himself down more stylishly than ever his critics did. Their presumed discomforture is accordingly part of the pleasure of the text.

The relationship between 'Mr Pinfold', the 'Evelyn Waugh' known to the public, and the 'real' author of *The Ordeal of Gilbert Pinfold* is thus what the novel is finally about. Not only is Mrs Pinfold a beautifully understated portrait of Waugh's wife, but Mr Pinfold's quiet submission to her demonstrates the underlying soundness of his own mind and heart. Additionally, she reinforces the novel's central claim about personal continuity and self-governance. But the novel contains another, more oblique set of references to Waugh's family. Waugh wrote some wonderful letters to his children, particularly to his daughter Margaret. He sent a farewell letter to her just before the journey to Ceylon – she was eleven at the time – and wrote to her again almost immediately on his return, telling her how sad it was being ill and alone in a foreign country. 'Perhaps', he added, 'when you are a proud prefect you will travel with me' (*Letters*, p. 422). 'Margaret' is of course the name of 'the General's' daughter who offers herself to Mr Pinfold in the novel; the 'General' not only urges his 'Meg, . . . [his] little Mimi' (p. 114) to learn the art of love from Mr Pinfold, he concludes, 'I'd like dearly to be the one myself to teach you, but you've made your own choice and who's to grudge it you?' In a book which so explicitly denigrates psychoanalysis, this careful adumbration of the theme of incest cannot be accidental. But it is certainly not confessional. Waugh is staring at an array of solemn, modern-minded boobies, and defying them to think the worst.

Yet at the same time his 'confessedly autobiographical novel' (*Essays*, p. 527) *is* a work of self-disclosure. At the end of his ordeal, Mr Pinfold is puzzled by the fact that he 'could make a far blacker and more plausible case' (p. 8) against himself than his persecutors did, even though, as the products of his own mind, they might have done so. A further implication of this insight, however, is that his persecutors' sadism, homophobia and anti-semitism are as much the products of his mind and heart as their ridiculous calumnies against him. In this connection, we may recall Cara's words in *Brideshead Revisited*: 'When people hate with all that energy, it is something in themselves they are hating.' (p. 99) If this expresses Waugh's view, the account of Mr Pinfold's delusions engages with the darkest aspects of Waugh's own life. The same may also be said of the other hate-filled pieces; in 'Tactical Exercise' and 'Love Among the Ruins', as in *The Ordeal of Gilbert Pinfold*, Waugh is addressing the problem of himself far more seriously than ever his critics did. The effect, however, is not of his baring his soul in public. *The Ordeal of Gilbert Pinfold* is sealed in on itself and is as protective of its author as *Black Mischief* or one of John Plant's detective novels. The real act of self-conquest which it discloses is Waugh's capacity to take the necropolis on the dark side of his mind and to treat it simply as

one more shapeless chunk of experience to be put into communicable form for the edification of readers like O'Brien. Mr Pinfold is a
mask – a mask moulded exactly to the contours of Waugh's face, but
a mask none the less, hard, bright and antiquated. The novel, far
from making its author a sitting shot to the world, serves rather to
enrich the public persona Waugh had created for himself, while
limiting and controlling those elements of explanation by which an
author's privacy is ultimately betrayed.

CHAPTER FIVE

Warriors:
Sword of Honour
(*Men at Arms, Officers and Gentlemen*
and *Unconditional Surrender*)

The three volumes which make up *Sword of Honour* address all the major themes of the post-war fiction in a final, complex arrangement of Waugh's thinking for a world-wide audience. This vast undertaking put his art and Faith decisively on trial, and gave him considerable trouble. Unlike *The Ordeal of Gilbert Pinfold*, it involved him in real acts of self-disclosure. Guy Crouchback is not a self-portrait like Mr Pinfold, but in talking uninhibitedly about 'the spiritual life', about salvation as a practical experience of the consciousness and the will, he and his father are drawn into the treacherous territory of explanation and justification. The piecemeal presentation of the work was another source of difficulty. The slow disclosure of Waugh's scheme made it easier for his critics to read the individual volumes in the light of their conception of his work as radically infected by neo-Jacobitism.

The narrative divides clearly in two: the first part is concluded at the end of *Officers and Gentlemen*, when the spirit of high farce and romanticized chivalry which sustain Guy through the first two years of the war finally fail him; the third volume, *Unconditional Surrender* (1961), deals with his spiritual revival and the successful reintegration of his life against the grain of developments in the public sphere.

These transitions are represented in a fundamental shift in the language of his conversation, thoughts and prayers. At the beginning of *Men at Arms* his life is empty. In a sociable community he is not *simpatico*: in the place where his grandparents found sexual joy, he is aridly celibate. His alienation is manifest in the confession he makes in Italian, a language he speaks 'well but without nuances'.

There was no risk of going deeper than the denunciation of his few infractions of law, of his habitual weaknesses. Into that wasteland where his soul languished he need not, could not, enter. He had no words to describe it. There were no words in any language. (p. 14)

But he is hardly less inhibited in English: first he cannot say ' "Here's how" to Major Tickeridge' (*Men at Arms*, p. 39), and even when he learns to do so he finds he cannot talk naturally to the Goan steward on the voyage to Dakar. He therefore takes refuge in a self-deceiving private rhetoric – 'Sir Roger, pray for me . . . and for our endangered kingdom' – a rhetoric as detached from the simple imperatives of fact as Gibbon's. His journey out of his spiritual Waste Land is the history of a mind struggling with language and truth.

Guy's problem is that the language of romance confuses his thinking about moral issues. In *Men at Arms*, when he is still stuck in Bellamy's, trying to get a posting, he finds that the failure of the Allies to react to the Russian invasion of Poland has little effect on older members who remember 'the mud and lice and noise' (p. 24) of the First World War – ' "Justice?" said the old soldiers. "Justice?" ' (p. 25) Again, when the Russians invade Finland, he is sickened by the thought 'that he was engaged in a war in which courage and a just cause were irrelevant to the issue' (p. 142), but his fellow Halberdiers are not concerned. Irrationally, his mood changes with the invasion of Norway –

he did not believe his country would lose this war; each apparent defeat seemed strangely to sustain it. There was in romance great virtue in unequal odds. There were in morals two requisites for a lawful war, a just cause and the chance of victory (p. 174)

and he goes to sleep contemplating the prospect of 'a whole new coastline . . . open for biffing' (p. 175). The mixture of languages – theological and schoolboy-romantic – is obviously suspect, but how Guy has gone wrong only becomes clear at the beginning of *Unconditional Surrender*. Utterly disillusioned by the declaration of war against Finland, he tells his father that he has lost interest in victory, to which Mr Crouchback retorts, 'Then you've no business to be a soldier' (p. 15). This reflects the Catholic teaching, recalled earlier by Guy, that war may only be fought in a just cause and provided the chances of success are reasonable. The individual soldier, however, cannot make comprehensive judgements about its conduct. Provided that he has reasonable grounds for believing the cause for which he is fighting is a good one, and that he does not participate in intrinsically wicked actions, such as the killing of hostages or the ill-treatment of prisoners, he should leave questions of strategy and general policy to the authorities: the declaration of war against Finland is thus not a question for soldiers. Guy's obsession with Justice on a global scale has been a form of hubris.

This is the context in which his relationship with the Halberdiers is best interpreted. Reviews of *Men at Arms* assumed that Guy's love affair with his regiment is unconditionally endorsed. Admittedly, the Halberdier tradition unites officers and men in bonds of loyalty and comradeship, but Guy allows himself to be seriously misled by the kitten games of tradition, by mere words – 'Gentlemen, these are the officers who will command you in battle' (*Men at Arms*, p. 136). The real language of the regiment (and that of Tommy Backhouse's Commandos) establishes humble truths which coordinate their attitudes and activities: that is why the Halberdiers are an efficient fighting force in Crete. (At another level it explains the success of 'Jumbo' Trotter's sybaritic odyssey.) And in his heart Guy knows that he and the Halberdiers speak different languages. His irreverent vision, as he marches past the parish church after Sunday Mass, of Sir Roger of Wraybrooke stepping out 'on his unaccomplished journey, leaving his madam padlocked' (*Men at Arms*, p. 63), is a sign of his lurking awareness of the disparity between his words and the Halberdiers' reality. So are his 'Truslove' fantasies on the Dakar expedition, which are shown up for what they are really worth by Ritchie-Hook's bloody little recce on to African soil. This process reaches its sorry conclusion in the story of Ivor Claire.

In a thoroughly unsympathetic review of *Unconditional Surrender*, Kingsley Amis claimed that Waugh was too forgiving towards the cowardly Claire (*Critical Heritage*, p. 420). He attributed this to a snobbish soft-heartedness on Waugh's part towards a glamorous upper-class character. But even before his disgrace in Crete, the language used of Ivor is subtly double-edged:

Guy remembered Claire as he first saw him in the Roman spring in the afternoon sunlight . . . putting his horse faultlessly over the jumps, concentrated as a man in prayer. Ivor Claire, Guy thought, was the fine flower of them all. He was quintessential England, the man Hitler had not taken into account, Guy thought. (*Officers and Gentlemen*, p. 114)

At this point Ivor personifies Guy's false vision of Chivalry and global Justice. The germ of this theme may have been planted in Waugh's mind by *God and the Atom*. Of the need in war–time to be right, Knox had written:

a man braces himself more readily for the moral struggle if he believes that right and wrong are easily distinguishable, and that the society to which he belongs adheres, at least in its major decisions, to the cause of right. (p. 16)

And of the need, or temptation, to idealize one's conduct:

Look at [war] . . . as one of the combatants, and . . . you see it as a Holy War . . . Having this good conceit of yourself, you instinctively fall back on a public attitude of scrupulous chivalry. (p. 62)

Such attitudes, Knox suggests, are not to be trusted. So does Waugh's prose. Bent over his horse's neck, Ivor only *looks* like a man at prayer. Yet it is not his disgrace but his rehabilitation which disabuses Guy of his dream, and in ways more complex than Amis suggests.

The key figure here is Julia Stitch, still plainly identifiable with Lady Diana Cooper, who was in Cairo during the evacuation from Crete. She and Tommy Backhouse, based more loosely on Sir Robert Laycock, to whom *Officers and Gentlemen* is dedicated, are prime agents in ensuring that Ivor's cowardice is kept under wraps. Full of the affability and vitality Guy lacks, they combine pragmatism and class loyalty in comfortably equal measure. But their 'simple rules of conduct' (p. 238) take no account of 'Justice', not the grand comprehensive principle with which Guy has been obsessed, but the personal, specific question of what might be due in practice to the men Ivor has deserted, 'Eddie and Bertie in prison . . . [and] the young soldier lying still unburied in the deserted village of Crete'.

Mrs Stitch can see nothing wrong in ruining Guy's military career to protect Ivor. Worse, she disposes of the dead soldier's identity disc without a thought to his family waiting for news of him.

This willingness of Guy's friends to pick up the baton of Ivor's dishonour acquires additional significance from its association with Stalin's entry into the war on the side of the allies. Guy was exhilarated by the Molotov-Ribbentrop Pact in 1939 because in uniting the two great atheistic dictatorships it appeared to make right and wrong easily distinguishable, and so to validate the ideal of chivalry in the sphere of personal conduct. Now all those certainties have gone: 'priests [are] spies and gallant friends [prove] traitors and his country [is] led blundering into dishonour' (p. 240). What happens to Ivor after that hardly matters. Waugh has inculpated far better than he in the moral myopia of expediency. He actually apologized to Lady Diana for giving her fictional counterpart this dubious role, but she replied 'that she did not mind at all, since she would have behaved in exactly the same way as Mrs Stitch' (*Diaries*, p. 797). The unknown soldier whose disc Mrs Stitch destroys is not a negligible figure, however:

Why was he lying there? Who were these girls? Had . . . they watched him die? Had they closed his eyes and composed his limbs? Guy would never know . . . Meanwhile, lacking words the three of them stood by the body, stiff and mute as figures in a sculptured Deposition. (p. 206)

This is the iconic sign which replaces Sir Roger in Guy's conscious-ness – a corpse attended by women like the dead Christ taken down from the Cross. Like others at Golgotha, Mrs Stitch evidently did not know what she was doing.

Had the narrative ended here, farce and romance would have been exposed as irrelevant in contemporary history and the structural pessimism of *Scott-King's Modern Europe* would have been mas-sively confirmed. That Guy's wartime career did not finish on this sad, sour note, however, can be confidently ascribed to five agents – Mr Crouchback, Guy himself, Virginia, Mme Kanyi and God.

Mr Crouchback was controversial from the start. Kingsley Amis was particularly exercised about the 'souped up traditionalism' (*Critical Heritage*, p. 422) in the account of his funeral in *Uncon-*

ditional Surrender. There is some substance to this charge, but Amis predictably misses the nuances in Waugh's treatment of neo-Jacobite motifs. Mr Crouchback does indeed come from very distinguished ancestry, but 'the massive and singular quality of [his] family pride' (*Men at Arms*, p. 34) is duly acknowledged, and there is carefully judged humour in the treatment of this side of his character. 'Every good house stands on a road or a river or a rock,' he tells his pupils. '. . . Only hunting-lodges belong in a park. It was after the Reformation that the new rich men began hiding away from the people' (*Officers and Gentlemen*, p. 22). This was calculated to infuriate critics like O'Brien and Amis. So were Miss Vavasour's indignation on Mr Crouchback's behalf – 'I very nearly interrupted them then and there, to tell them *who you are* . . .' (p. 24) – and Mr Goodall's vision of neo-Jacobitism on a European scale:

> led by the priests and squires, with blessed banners, and the relics of saints borne ahead, Poles, Hungarians, Austrians, Bavarians, Italians and plucky little contingents from the Catholic cantons of Switzerland would soon be on the march to redeem the times. (p. 40)

But Amis is right to this extent: Mr Crouchback's difficulties in the hotel set up a tendentious antithesis between (wealthy) Catholic gentility and the acquisitive *petit bourgeoisie*, while his funeral in *Unconditional Surrender* is a dauntingly reverent celebration of the faded if exclusive glories of Recusancy.

There is more to this scene than reverence, however. A trap is laid for Mr Crouchback's family pride in *Sword of Honour*, and it reaches a crucial stage at his funeral. In important respects this outcome must be seen, like that of *Brideshead Revisited*, as the work of divine Providence. Providence is never an easy theme in literature, because it is so readily confused with chance and luck, particularly in an age when even Catholics were finding the idea a difficult one. As Knox pointed out in *God and the Atom*, belief in special providences – strong in the eighteenth century – had declined in the nineteenth into the generalized, secular notions about the 'providential' underlying the theories of evolution and progress, and even these were beginning to seem unrealistic after a world war which ended with area bombing of civilian targets, and the abandonment of Central Europe to the armies of Stalin. Providence was thus a dangerous theme for a novelist to work with and some key incidents in Waugh's treatment of it were subject to misreading by early reviewers.

This was particularly so of Guy's attempt to seduce his divorced wife, Virginia, in *Men at Arms*, which was condemned as being 'like a scene from some shabby and tasteless bedroom farce' (*Critical Heritage*, p. 340). Amis thought Waugh would 'have to pull round a lot to efface the memory of that scene' (*Critical Heritage*, p. 374). What these early critics could not foresee was that this incident initiates a complex meditation on Providence, which is only concluded with the resentful remark of Arthur Box-Bender's at the very end of *Unconditional Surrender*: 'Yes . . . things have turned out very conveniently for Guy' (p. 240).

The attempted seduction is prompted by Mr Goodall's story of a childless Catholic nobleman becoming the lover of his former wife and begetting a son who is accepted by his mother's second husband, inherits the latter's title, and marries a Catholic. In consequence an ancient, apparently extinct Catholic family continues under another name and in the old Faith. 'Explain it how you will,' says Mr Goodall, 'I see the workings of Providence there' (p. 120). Guy is sceptical about a providential concern 'with the perpetuation of the English Catholic aristocracy' but Mr Goodall reminds him of the saying about the fall of a sparrow. In the case of the Crouchback family, however, Providence reverses this scheme. Guy will not be the father of his ex-wife's child, and the heir to an ancient Catholic name will thus be a hair-dresser's bastard. In the earlier version of *Unconditional Surrender* Guy has two sons by his second marriage, but in the final recension of *Sword of Honour*, little Trimmer is his sole heir.

This is a remarkable outcome, but it does not meet the subtler objections of Waugh's critics. Virginia's baby, after all, will be expensively educated by the Benedictine Community in which his cousin, Tony, is a monk. The Crouchback ethos will thus be handed on: a formal gesture towards egalitarian principle *sub specie aeternitatis* effectively ensures that this side of eternity things turn out very conveniently for the upper classes and the Catholic Church. Endings, however (as Waugh's revisions show), are arbitrary things – his critics, after all, did not spare him when he left his Catholic characters in worldly desolation at the end of *Brideshead Revisited*. The issue is rather one of means – how things turn out conveniently for Guy and for other characters also.

Amis objected to the disappearance of Trimmer at the end of *Unconditional Surrender* as well as to the rehabilitation of Ivor. This is a minor fault, for though Trimmer is the personification of vulgarity in the ascendant, he is not the agent of his own advancement. An important moment occurs in *Officers and Gentlemen* when Ian Kilbanock tells Guy that Tommy Backhouse's men are not good propaganda material precisely because they are

'. . . the "Fine Flower of the Nation". You can't deny it and *it won't do* . . . This is a People's War . . . and the People won't have . . . flowers. Flowers stink. The upper classes are on the secret list . . .' (p. 101)

These words are full of unwitting truth. Ian's remark about flowers stinking will prove prophetic with respect to Ivor, while Guy himself is already on the list being compiled by Grace-Groundling-Marchpole. Finally in identifying Trimmer as a suitable hero, Ian will connive in the extinction of his own class. In small matters as in great, he is a shabby careerist: he tricks Guy into proposing the Air Marshal for membership of Bellamy's in *Men at Arms* and he acts as Trimmer's procurer in *Unconditional Surrender*. He then proposes palming off Trimmer's baby on Guy. By contrast, Trimmer is a cheeky coward, an unabashed womaniser, and in Virginia's case a helpless romantic. It is not the common man who is responsible for his own apotheosis in *Sword of Honour*, but Lord Kilbannock, whose self-proclaimed ambition is 'to be known as one of the soft-faced men who did well out of the war' (*Men at Arms*, p. 26). In objecting to Trimmer's disappearance at the end of *Unconditional Surrender*, Amis fails to note that things also turn out very conveniently for Ian.

His other complaint was against the 'souped up traditionalism'

which surrounds Mr Crouchback. The problem with Mr Crouchback is that he is a saint. He is meant to be, as Knox put it, one of
'those to whom a sense of God's existence is most vivid, holy people
[who] seem to achieve both a lightness of heart and a lightness of
touch which indicates that their lives are integrated' (*God and the
Atom*, p. 15). Like Guy, he is a romantic – he is completely taken in
by the propaganda about Trimmer – but unlike Guy, he puts his
trust not in heroes but in God. At the funeral, Guy recalls how Mr
Crouchback 'had suffered as much as most men – more perhaps –
from bad news of one kind or another; never fearfully' (*Unconditional Surrender*, p. 64). Of such people, Knox writes, 'If only we
knew, we others, what it feels like to have solid confidence in God!
Concerned about the future of mankind they certainly are; worried
they certainly are not' (*God and the Atom*, p. 139).

God and the Atom ends with the suggestion that we need the
presence of saints in our lives. In his father Guy was granted such a
presence, 'the only entirely good man, he had ever known'. In his last
conversation with Mr Crouchback, Guy is instructed not only in the
principles governing a soldier's conduct in war, but in the nature of
Providence. The topic arises when Guy remarks that the Lateran
Treaty of 1929 between the Pope and Mussolini had been a mistake.
If only the Pope had stood out a little longer, Guy says. His father
calls this nonsense; Guy has not considered 'how many souls may
have been reconciled and have died at peace as a result of [the
Treaty] . . . Quantitative judgements don't apply. If only one soul
was saved that is full compensation for any amount of loss of
"face" ' (p. 17). This echoes Knox's views in *God and the Atom*:
'the imagination,' he writes, 'discipline it as we may, is daunted by
high totals' (p. 51). 'God's scale of values is [not] a replica of the
scale of values we take for granted' (p. 59).

Guy recalls this conversation at the funeral, and it prompts him to
think carefully about himself, about 'the deadly core of his apathy
. . . Enthusiasm and activity were not enough. God required more
than that. He had commanded all men to *ask*' (p. 66). Guy then
makes the fundamental act of the will on which the entire action
turns:

One day he would get the chance to do some small service which only he could perform . . . He did not expect a heroic destiny. Quantitative judgements did not apply . . . Perhaps his father was at that moment clearing the way for him. 'Show me what you want me to do and help me to do it,' he prayed.

This prayer, which is apparently 'directed to . . . his father' as an earlier prayer had been directed to Sir Roger, is answered in due course: Guy's vocation is to be little Trimmer's foster-father. Mr Crouchback's heavenly intercession is thus one of the means, under God, by which things turn out conveniently for little Trimmer. The great celebration of traditional Catholic Englishry to which Amis objected is also the moment at which pride of descent is subverted, and the agent of that subversion is literally the holy old man who felt it in life with such quiet intensity.

It is as a result of his experience at his father's funeral that Guy is able to redefine his sense of chivalry. Clearly, 'being *chivalrous* – about *Virginia*' (p. 151) is not the kind of knight errantry he dreamt about beside Sir Roger's tomb. As the furious Kerstie Killbannock tells him, it is an action which sensible people would regard as insane. Guy agrees: it is 'not the normal behaviour of an officer and gentleman'; it is 'something they'll laugh about in Bellamy's'. But chivalry does not deal in high totals either. Like Justice, it is not a grand abstract principle but something that is owed in practice to individuals like Eddie and Bertie in prison and the young unburied soldier in Crete, or in this case an unborn, fatherless child.

For Guy, it also has the happy worldly consequence of restoring his manhood. In the sour bleakness of war-time Britain, Virginia is a manifestation of integration at the level of the flesh, as Mr Crouchback is a manifestation of integration at the level of the spirit. Even in contexts of waste-land seediness, she refreshes and enlivens, above all in the unaffected freedom with which she uses language. She is at a particularly low point, for example, when Trimmer picks her up in Glasgow, but the moment he identifies himself as her hairdresser on the *Aquitania* she comes to life: 'Gustave, how awful of me! How could I have forgotten? Sit down. You must admit you've changed a lot' (*Officers and Gentlemen*,

p. 75). Guy would have been incapable of such linguistic ease. She is equally relaxed when Kerstie tells her that her prospective abortionist is black: ' "Why should I mind?" asked Virginia' (*Unconditional Surrender*, p. 80). She is reunited with Guy (and accepted back into the family by the misty-eyed Peregrine) largely as a consequence of the directness and honesty with which she speaks to them.

Her subsequent relations with Guy are only described after he has received the news of her death.

> The news did not affect Guy greatly . . . The answer to the question that had agitated Kerstie Kilbannock (and others of his acquaintance) – what had been his relations with Virginia . . . ? – was simple enough . . . Virginia . . . with gentle, almost tender, agility adapted her endearments to his crippled condition . . . Without passion or sentiment but in a friendly, cosy way they had resumed the pleasures of marriage and in the weeks while his knee mended the deep old wound in Guy's heart and pride healed also . . . When Guy was passed fit for active service . . . he had felt as though he were leaving a hospital where he had been skillfully treated, a place of grateful memory to which he had no particular wish to return. (p. 196)

This is a decidedly unsentimental note of valediction. It is also, however, a sharp reminder that Virginia's death is yet another of the ways in which things turn out very conveniently for Guy. It is therefore a matter which requires detailed consideration.

At least two major themes besides that of providence converge in the narrative of Virginia's death – language and truth and the death wish. All three are also in play in the related study of Ludovic and his writings, which in an odd way provides the key to Waugh's entire design.

Ludovic's story is a curious reversal of Guy's. Thus for all their pretentiousness, Ludovic's jottings in *Officers and Gentlemen* contain some acute insights:

> '*Captain Crouchback,*' Corporal-Major Ludovic noted, '*is pleased because General Miltiades is a gentleman. He would like to believe that the war is being fought by such people. But all gentlemen are now very old.*' (p. 186)

He even includes Cara's great insight among his *aperçus*:

'*Man is what he hates . . . Yesterday I was Blackhouse. Today I am Crouchback. Tomorrow, merciful heaven, shall I be Hound?*' (p. 121)

After Crete, however, Ludovic loses his ability to bring language and truth together. At the parachute training school in *Unconditional Surrender*, his writing becomes unmistakably Gibbon-like:

The further he removed from human society and the less he attended to human speech, the more did words . . . occupy his mind. The books he read were books about words . . . He dreamed of words ands woke repeating them . . . Ludovic had become an addict of that potent intoxicant, the English language. (pp. 38–9)

He ends up writing like an automaton:

Lady Marmaduke was a bitch. Ludovic had known from the start that she must die in the last chapter. He made no plans . . . He waited to see, as he might have sat in a seat at the theatre watching the antics of the players over whom he had no control. (p. 188)

This is not unlike Waugh's own experience as an artist, notably when he was developing Angela Lyne's character in *Put Out More Flags*, but in his case writing demanded deliberate re-writing once the basic material had been supplied by experience or inspiration. Typically, in *Unconditional Surrender*, he plays a kitten game with both Ludovic and Virginia of a kind Ludovic would never have dreamt of playing with Lady Marmaduke: he makes Ludovic's first book a sly parody of Cyril Connolly's *The Unquiet Grave*, and gives his second the same title as Book Three of *Unconditional Surrender*, as well as a style that sounds mischievously like that of both *Brideshead Revisited* and *The Unquiet Grave*, a hedonistic evocation of 'the odorous gardens of a recent past transformed and illuminated by disordered memory and imagination'. Later Everard Spruce gives his secretaries a mini-tutorial on how Virginia was a literary type, similar to the heroines of Aldous Huxley and Ernest Hemingway, until one of them exclaims that the character he is describing 'sounds more like the heroine of Major Ludovic's dreadful *Death Wish*' (p. 200). Comparisons are evidently being invited. But this is not the first occasion on which intertextuality is discreetly highlighted in *Sword of Honour*. At the end of *Men at Arms*, Guy is said to have amused himself years later with the thought that while waiting with the Halberdiers in Africa he might have gone to confession to a priest in Graham Greene's *The Heart of the Matter*. The observation passes almost unnoticed, but as Waugh had observed in 1938, 'writing is an art which exists in a time sequence; each sentence and each page is dependent on its predecessors and successors; a sentence . . . may owe its significance to another fifty pages distant' (*Essays*, p. 239). Or to others two volumes distant. Recalling the reference to Greene, or noticing it on re-reading, is thus a reminder of the difference between a Waugh-text and a Ludovic-text, that the former involves the overt patterning of incident, character and phrase, and the latter is a kind of automatic writing. Virginia's death is certainly not like Lady Marmaduke's, something that her author instinctively wishes on her, but part of a carefully developed design by which the ending of *Men at Arms* is replayed with significant variations at the end of *Unconditional Surrender*.

This is done in small matters and in great. Immediately after the casual allusion to *The Heart of the Matter* in *Men at Arms*, for example, we learn, just as parenthetically, of Leonard's death:

Leonard was still on the strength of the Second Battalion, pending posting. It was now announced that he was dead, killed by a bomb, on leave in South London. (p. 232)

This casual piece of authorial spite against Mrs Leonard, for keeping her husband at home, acquires additional significance when, again two volumes later, the falling of two further bombs is linked to the theme of Providence. The first kills Virginia, Peregrine and Mrs Corner; the second passes over Everard Spruce and his secretaries as they discuss Virginia and Lady Marmaduke, and over Eloise Plessington and Angela Box-Bender as they discuss Virginia and Providence. The latter agree that Virginia's death was probably a good thing. '. . . There's a special providence in the fall of a bomb,' says Eloise, deliberately misquoting Hamlet as well as Christ,

'. . . She was killed at the one time in her life when she could be sure of heaven – eventually.' She then offers to take little Gervase – he will be an interest for her daughter, Domenica. (Domenica will be Guy's second wife.) Finally they become aware of the bomb and Angela prays that it will be a dud and not explode at all. But it does – 'in a street already destroyed by earlier bombs and now quite deserted'.

Is this a case of prayer being answered? The faithful would say yes, that God takes all the prayers of his people into account when arranging his universe, but that this cannot be shown, his scale of values not being a replica of ours. It would be inappropriate therefore for Waugh to introduce any suggestion of the miraculous into his text, as Greene did in another novel, *The End of the Affair*. But it would be a betrayal of the Catholic thrust of the trilogy for Waugh to cast doubt on the efficacy of prayer. So, having killed off first Leonard, then Peregrine's entire household with bombs, he puts a prayer and the harmless third bomb side by side, and presents them stony-faced to a sceptical readership. 'We go on praying for individual benefits,' Knox writes of his fellow-Catholics in *God and the Atom*, 'and feel grateful over them . . . But our public attitude . . . is to hope rather for the wide distribution of good things than for their accurate canalization' (p. 51). Yet the principle of entrusting those we love 'to God's safe-keeping' (p. 58), he insists, is the same in the age of the atom bomb 'as in the old, primitive days of the rocket-bomb'.

But the full meaning of the assertion that there is a special providence in the fall of a bomb only emerges from the narrative of Virginia's death, in which everything is again meticulously planned. The cattiness in Eloise's observation that Virginia will have a long stretch in Purgatory is off-set in advance by a remark of Peregrine's that Virginia was 'a much jollier sort of convert than people like Eloise Plessington' (p. 185). More important is Kerstie's remark about Virginia's dislike of the baby. '. . . In a novel or a film,' she says, 'the baby ought to make Virginia a changed character. It hasn't . . .' (p. 189). The chapter ends with Virginia and Angela agreeing that Gervase should go to the country with Angela and Virginia waits in London:

So it was arranged and Virginia comfortably recuperated as the bombs chugged overhead and she wondered, as each engine cut out: 'Is that the one that's coming here?' (p. 191)

The next we hear of Virginia is in her letter to Guy, in which she refers to the baby as 'it' and Eloise as her great new friend, and Angela's letter announcing her death.

Few major works of fiction can depend so decisively on such an unobtrusively placed definite article. 'Is that the one that's coming here?' Virginia, like all the other characters, has some kind of death wish. She is waiting fatalistically for the bomb with her name on it. Perhaps that is why she rejects the baby. More probably she just dislikes it. In either case her decision to stay in London suggests that in some sense she is choosing to die – because there is really no future for Guy and herself, because her hold on her religion is so tenuous. In one way or another, the providential fall of her bomb is intimately yet unreadably involved with the mystery of her very human will.

Things, then, turn out conveniently for Guy because his own choices and those of his father and his wife play their small parts in the weave of the divine text. One thing more remains to be done, however. The clear implication of Guy's last conversation with his father is that his entire military career has been a sin, a sin for which he will only obtain absolution when he has learned to speak more fully about himself than he did to the priest at Santa Dulcina. He goes to confession regularly thereafter, but never, in human terms, very fruitfully. In Africa he confesses to 'increasing sloth, one dismal occasion of drunkenness, and the lingering resentment he felt at the injustice he had suffered in . . . "Operation Truslove" ' (*Men at Arms*, p. 232); in Cairo his confessor is a spy, his confession trivial; in Italy again, the priest will not even recognize his death wish as a sin. (Almost simultaneously, Virginia makes her good and humble first confession – 'fully, accurately, without extenuation or elaboration. The recital of half a life-time's mischief [takes] less than five minutes') (*Unconditional Surrender*, p. 171). But Guy does succeed in confessing his sins at last, though only after Mme Kanyi has completed the work which Mr Crouchback began:

'Is there any place that is free from evil? [she asks] It is too simple to say that only the Nazis wanted war. These communists wanted it too. It was the only way in which they could come to power. Many of my people wanted it, to be revenged on the Germans, to hasten the creation of the national state. It seems to me there was a will to war, a death wish, everywhere. Even good men thought their private honour would be satisfied by war . . .'

'God forgive me,' said Guy. 'I was one of them.' (p. 232)

Here, finally, language and reality come together for Guy: Mme Kanyi's words are full of the grace and truth he needs. At 'the end of a long war', Knox writes in *God and the Atom*, '. . . the clean sheet must be a white sheet of penitence, even if we are inclined to blame our elders for it' (p. 17). It is only in the wake of such an act of penitence that things turn out very conveniently for Guy, and the person who brings this about (under God) is a woman for whose death he is indirectly responsible. Providence is not a soft narrative option in *Sword of Honour*.

The murder of the Kanyis provides yet another link between the endings of the first and third volumes of the trilogy. The triviality of the charge against them, and the casual manner in which Guy comes to hear of their execution, are deeply troubling. The episode makes the high spirits of the Epilogue particularly difficult to justify. This can only be done by reading *Sword of Honour* carefully as an historical novel.

Mrs Kanyi's speech makes it clear that the death wish underlying both Guy's romantic view of the war and his subsequent disillusionment were manifestations of the spirit of the age. His painful transformation, however, is not matched by any developments in the public sphere, but is set against the entry of the Soviet Union into the war, the forging of the Stalingrad sword, and the Teheran Conference, which is in session when he makes his decision to take Virginia back. (The Teheran Conference, the text reminds us, was 'entirely occupied with quantitative judgements' (*Unconditional Surrender*, p. 128) — judgements which led to the great betrayals represented in the novel by the Jugoslavian narrative in general, and the murder of the Kanyis in particular.) Thus paradoxically the restoration of Guy's capacity to involve himself in the world is a consequence of his learning to resist the mental background of the times. His spiritual and moral success becomes a measure of the world's failure and a sign of the concealed counterthrust of the divine plan.

Guy, of course, is not the only historical signifier in the text. The moral bankruptcy of British political life, for example, is embodied in Arthur Box-Bender and the senior of the Grace-Groundling-Marchpole brothers. Box-Bender represents the modern Conservative Party which Waugh so heartily despised. (Labour politicians hardly appear in his fiction, except as background characters; they are all ex-Communists or fellow-travellers like Gilpin, who is elected at the 1945 election when Box-Bender loses his seat.) Box-Bender's one acute and appalling political observation concerns the Soviet advances after Stalingrad in 1943 – '. . . Everything is going merrily on the eastern front,' he tells Guy. '. . . Uncle Joe's fairly got them on the run. I shouldn't much care to be one of his prisoners' (*Unconditional Surrender*, p. 48). Grace-Groundling-Marchpole is the great red herring of the trilogy. His pursuit of Guy is futile and his tolerance of de Souza complacent. That the entire exercise achieves nothing except to keep Guy out of Italy where he might have been useful is of course the point. What does emerge from this aspect of the narrative is the unnerving accuracy of some of Waugh's guesses about the world of Intelligence, for it is hardly possible that Sir Ralph Brompton was actually based on the then Sir Anthony Blunt, whom he nevertheless so much resembles.

Two characters with greater political significance are the American, Loot, and Frank de Souza, the Jewish Communist. Together they function as representatives of the powers that were apparently to inherit the earth in 1945. Loot is an unexpected embodiment of American perspectives. He is the antithesis of the naïve Californians of *The Loved One*. Urbane and ubiquitous, he combines the ruthlessness of a New York lawyer with the cultural omnivorousness of the East Coast intellectual. But his engagement with artistic, social and personal values is as trivial as that of Wilbur Kenworthy, and less honest. His position at the end of *Unconditional Surrender* as Ludovic's factotum suggests that he may be homosexual; otherwise he seems devoid of human feelings. He is not so much a representative American as a portent of the triviality of success in the modern world. If any political or historical significance attaches to his valueless know-how and self-confidence it derives from the contrast between his lack of direction or horizons and the vision and purpose informing the career of Frank de Souza.

De Souza is a remarkably understated but impressive conception. Waugh's presentation of 'the communist conspiracy' is angry but controlled and in its way respectful. The picture of de Souza is built up slowly over the three volumes. In *Men at Arms* he is a figure in the background with Leonard and Sarum-Smith, one of the group of Halberdier officers overshadowed by Apthorpe, but he makes a stronger impression than the others because he is so obviously intelligent. He is the only Halberdier with the wit and education to greet Guy with a quotation from *Hamlet*: 'Oh my prophetic soul, my uncle' (p. 79). He is 'a dark, reserved, drily humorous, efficient young man', and he and his charmless companion at the theatre make a 'cold odd couple'. He is no more conspicuous or less memorable when Guy meets him again in Crete, with his wounded ear, his coolness under pressure and his bitter sense of probable German tactics.

In *Unconditional Surrender* Waugh skilfully brings Guy into contact with all the Communist characters – Sir Ralph Brompton at the Hazardous Offensive Operations Headquarters, de Souza and Gilpin, first at Ludovic's training establishment, where de Souza's mischief-making is singularly joyless, then in Bari and Begoy where 'in the whirligig of war' (p. 193) de Souza becomes Guy's commanding officer, giving him orders with the easy courtesy of a man who learned his service manners with the Halberdiers. None of Waugh's Communists is a monster: Suzie at HOO HQ and Major Catermole the 'transformed' Fellow of All Souls in Bari are quite commonplace. When the plane bringing Ben Ritchie-Hook, Ian Kilbannock and their party to the demonstration attack on the Croatian nationalists crashes near Begoy, de Souza says chillingly 'That's the end of *them*' (p. 217) – it is the nearest he comes to atrocity. He and his friends simply use the whirligig of war as Providence uses it, for their own secret purposes. At the end of the conversation about the Mass Guy has had said for Virginia, de Souza reminds him that this is not the time for sectarian loyalties. 'You wouldn't call communism a sect?'

asks Guy, and de Souza answers, 'No.' He begins to say more, stops, and then repeats ' "No" with absolute assurance' (p. 206). It is a moment of mutual understanding such as Guy could never experience with any other non-Catholic character. The historical process has resolved itself into a struggle between the only institutions with a clear sense of history and a universal mission – Communism and Catholicism, each in its way a child of Judaism – and between the two characters representing them, de Souza and Guy.

From the moment he joins the Halberdiers to our last glimpse of him as one of the Commando dinner party in the Epilogue stumbling noisily down the staircase at Bellamy's, Guy differs from de Souza not just in his beliefs but also in his appetite for fun, without which the trilogy could not have been what it undoubtedly is – a comedy. It is in the relation of this comedy to Catholicism that the paradox of Guy's conveniently happy ending discloses its meaning. To understand that meaning, therefore, we need to consider the two major comic characters of *Men at Arms*, Ben Ritchie-Hook and Apthorpe.

Ritchie-Hook is a daemon-possessed vehicle of the death wish, of what Bataille calls 'the free play of innocence' (p. 6), 'the puerile but discreet scandal of caprice and sovereign humour' (p. 133), the 'instinctive tendency towards divine intoxication which the rational world of calculation cannot bear . . . to which the instincts of childhood are closely related' (p. 9) and which merges with Death in opposing 'those intentions of Good which are based on rational calculation' (p. 11):

'. . . There's a limit to the amount of training men can take . . . Use them,' he repeated dreamily, 'spend them. It's like slowly collecting a pile of chips and then plonking them all down on the roulette board. It's the most fascinating thing in life, training men and staking them against the odds . . . you throw them into action and in a week, perhaps in a few hours the whole thing is expended . . .' (*Men at Arms*, p. 70)

This, refreshingly free of the stylistic solemnity of the French, is precisely what Bataille means by 'sovereignty'. Thus, though it is firmly put in its place in *Helena*, and manfully overcome in *The Ordeal of Gilbert Pinfold*, Evil in this special sense courses through the first half of the trilogy with a freedom that might have given even

Dennis Barlow pause, notably when Ritchie-Hook lays a coconut in Guy's lap, in the shape of 'the wet, curly head of a Negro' (*Men at Arms*, p. 227). After Crete, however, Guy's world is peopled by serious adults like Gilpin and de Souza. When he and Ritchie-Hook meet again, Evil, Death and Sovereignty are seen to be aspects, after all, of a fallen world. 'The sovereign attitude', writes Bataille, 'is guilty, miserable in so far as it tries to flee from death, but just as it dies, the wild feeling of childhood is again suffused with useless liberty' (p. 139). That seems to have been what Ritchie-Hook was seeking, but we need also to bear in mind the words of the badly burnt Dawkins: '. . . One thing for him; different for me that's got a wife and kids and was twenty years younger' (*Unconditional Surrender*, p. 223).

The affinity between 'Operation Truslove' and the wretched assault on the Croatian nationalists' little fort is a further example of how carefully the foundations of the third volume are laid in the first. A similar comparison unsettles in retrospect the story of Apthorpe. Apthorpe is a variation on the theme of Atwater, and is the perfect foil to Ritchie-Hook. Like Atwater and Don Quixote he carries a manifest burden of personal unhappiness, without which his contest with the Brigadier for control of the Thunder Box would simply be childish. By locating this contest in the scene of Apthorpe's prep-school days Waugh keeps his narrative in touch with the humiliations of an inept and lonely childhood, yet it remains comic because Apthorpe now has defences which almost match those of Grimes. But it is a close-run thing, especially in the African hospital, when he attempts to smoke in order to be companionable, and Guy sees tears on his colourless cheeks. Apthorpe, however, has resources even *in extremis*: he confesses to lying about the aunt in Peterborough, giggling 'slightly at his cleverness like Mr Toad in *The Wind in the Willows*' (*Men at Arms*, p. 237), and when he bequeaths his gear to Chatty Corner, Apthorpe gallantly saves the text from pathos:

> '. . . You'll do that for me, won't you, old man?'
> 'Very well. I'll try.'

'Then I can die happy – at least if anyone ever does die happy. Do you think they do?'

'We used to pray for it a lot at school. But for goodness' sake don't start thinking of dying *now*.'

'I'm a great deal nearer death now,' said Apthorpe, suddenly huffy, 'than you ever were at school.' (pp. 238–9)

He goes out as he came in, his defences gamely up, and the way is thus clear for Colonel Hector Campbell and his mad niece to keep alive the spirit of violence and lunacy in *Officers and Gentlemen*. In retrospect, however, Apthorpe's death chillingly anticipates the end of Guy's third adventure in Jugoslavia. His confession to Guy is a prospective parody of Guy's to Mrs Kanyi, and Guy's fatal gift of whisky foreshadows the even more innocent gift of magazines to the Kanyis which results in their execution. The world in 1945 recapitulates careless farce as shabby tragedy. When Guy returns to England at the end of 'The Death Wish' the spirit of comedy seems as dead as Ben Ritchie-Hook.

How, then, can Guy's ebullience in the Epilogue be justified? At the level of history, it cannot be: the results of the war in Europe had seen to that. Hence the disdainful irony of the Epilogue's opening sentence: 'In 1951, to celebrate the opening of a happier decade, the Government decreed a Festival.' But in *God and the Atom*, Knox had written that the 'Christian virtue of hope [had] nothing to do with the world's future' (p. 104); whatever the state of the times, hope remained 'something that [was] demanded of us' even if it meant only '*behaving as if we hoped*' (p. 107). The task Waugh seems to have set himself was to confront what Knox called the 'discouraging . . . portents of our times' (p. 113), by enabling Guy to do just that.

The party at Bellamy's is a reunion of Tommy Backhouse's commandos on Mugg, and it is the spirit of that time which the Epilogue fleetingly revives. After dining with Tommy at the Laird's castle on his first evening on Mugg, Guy found himself sharing a mood of wild elation with the man who had taken his wife and was now his commanding officer:

Tommy and Guy were indeed inebriated, not solely, nor in the main, by what they had drunk. They were caught up and bowled over by that sacred wind which once blew freely over the young world. Cymbals and flutes rang in their ears. (*Officers and Gentlemen*, p. 68)

Guy returns to this condition fairly frequently. It draws him to Apthorpe and draws Ritchie-Hook to him; all three have access to a schoolboy world – a place of primitive anxiety but also of happy carelessness about the future, and of something more important. For the world of irresponsible fun is more than it seems. The sacred wind which blows across Mugg is plainly pagan, but Book One of *Officers and Gentlemen* opens with a description of a bombing raid on London. Guy is reminded first of a Turner skyscape, then of the great liturgical celebration of Holy Saturday, which begins with the lighting of a new fire, and finally of a pentecostal wind. When he goes on to Bellamy's (where Air Marshal Beech is hiding under the billiard table) he hears preposterous stories of the streets running with whisky and brandy, or with wine; even war can evoke sacramental imagery. This motif reappears at the beginning of Book Two, when Major-General Whale's unhappy interview at the War Office on Holy Saturday morning coincides with the singing of the *Exultet* in Westminster Cathedral. Waugh is evidently pointing to an aspect of religion which his emphasis on the reasonableness of Christianity has tended to obscure – that the goal of the spiritual life is ecstasy. The presence of this theme in the trilogy radically qualifies the distinction between Evil and the world of humble truths which I have been labouring.

Intoxicating winds only blow intermittently through Guy's life after Mugg. His friendship with Ivor is not playful; his teasing of Major Hound in Cairo, his wild shopping expedition with Julia Stitch and his drive back to camp with the Commander-in-Chief briefly restore the spirit of Kut-al-Imara House and Mugg, but they also prepare the ground for the disaster of Crete, and his subsequent disillusionment in Cairo. In *Unconditional Surrender*, as we have seen, the innocence of *Men at Arms* is replayed as savagely bitter experience. War no longer evokes images of pentecostal fire; a flying-bomb raid on the contrary is a reminder of the Plagues of Egypt:

It was something quite other than the battle scene of the blitz with its drama of attack and defence; its earth-shaking concentrations of destruction and roaring furnaces . . . It was as impersonal as a plague, as though the city were infested with enormous, venemous insects. (p. 190)

There are, however, two moments in *Unconditional Surrender* when Guy glimpses beatitude once more. The first is when he makes his parachute jump:

The hazy November sun enveloped him in golden light. His solitude was absolute.
He experienced rapture, something as near as his earthbound soul could reach to a foretaste of paradise, *locum refrigerii, lucis et pacis*. The aeroplane seemed as far distant as will, at the moment of death, the spinning earth . . . He was a free spirit in an element as fresh as on the day of its creation.
All too soon the moment of ecstasy ceased. He was not suspended motionless; he was falling fast. (pp. 102–3)

The Latin ('place of cool repose, of light and of peace') is from the prayer for the dead in the Canon of the Mass. Guy's second glimpse of beatitude occurs in Begoy, when the Jewish refugees receive their long-delayed supplies. As in the Brighton scenes in *A Handful of Dust*, a potentially anti-semitic allusion to the stereotype of the ostentatious Jew yields to an exactly stated gesture of respect:

For the next few days a deplorable kind of ostentation seemed to possess the Jews. A curse seemed to have been lifted. They appeared everywhere, trailing the skirts of their great-coats in the snow, stamping their huge new boots, gesticulating with their gloved hands. Their faces shone with soap, they were full of Spam and dehydrated fruits. They were a living psalm. And then, as suddenly, they disappeared. (p. 229)

Both these occasions of holy joy are abruptly concluded. From the point of view of Guy's spiritual development, the second, placed immediately before his moment of epiphany with Mme Kanyi, is the more important.
It seems to be an aspect of this development that, except for the essentially private experience at his father's Requiem Mass, all his

contacts with the official Church from 1939 until the end of the war should be fruitless in human terms. Ultimate supernatural reality is certainly not presented in the trilogy on the great open altars of Catholic Europe. Instead obscure significations of the natural order – fire and air working on Guy's isolated consciousness during a bombing raid or a parachute descent – and the actions and words of Mme Kanyi and her companions in Begoy become surrogates in his mind for the Bible and the priesthood, for Word and Sacrament. The Jews of Begoy, without in any way relinquishing their Judaism, or having it diminished, are the only perfect sign of Catholic Christianity (Mr Crouchback excepted) in the entire trilogy. They are the means by which Guy rediscovers Christian hope, a hope which has nothing to do with worldly well-being, and which cannot be extinguished, therefore, even by the cruelty of the Kanyis' execution. 'Spiritually,' Pope Pius XI told a group of Belgian Catholics in 1938, 'we are semites' (*Encyclopaedia Judaica*, XIII, col. 573). It was a lesson Guy Crouchback was to learn from Mme Kanyi and her companions in Begoy in 1944.

Sword of Honour enters the treacherous territory of explanation and justification, therefore, only to clarify the problems it addresses – Providence, the human will, the divine promises; it does not depend on explanation or tendentious plotting to resolve them. It expresses a vision of human possibility and divine hope in formal rather than expository terms. Its engagement with history is deeply meditated and (in a non-academic sense) authentically philosophical, but its procedures are paradigmatic not discursive. It is thus a work in the neo-classical manner, in which meaning is inseparable from 'Design'. In the Preface to *Fables Ancient and Modern* (1700), John Dryden, like Waugh a Catholic conservative dismayed to find himself out of tune with the politics of his age, described the way such literature functions. In answer to Thomas Hobbes's assertion that the first beauty of an epic poem is its diction – a view which Ludovic would have readily endorsed – Dryden wrote:

Now, the Words are the Colouring of the Work, which in the Order of Nature is last to be consider'd. The Design, the Disposition, the Manners, and the Thoughts, are all before it: Where any of these are wanting or imperfect, so much wants or is imperfect in the imitation of Humane Life; which is in the very Definition of a Poem. (*The Poems and Fables of John Dryden*, pp. 524–5)

Or of a novel. And few modern English novels vindicate these principles so triumphantly as *Sword of Honour*.

Conclusion

In bringing the trilogy to a successful and happy conclusion, Waugh had been obeying Knox's injunction to go on behaving – in his case writing – as if he hoped. In fact he was near despair. He was enraged beyond measure by changes in the Catholic Church: the great chant '*Quomodo sedet sola civitas*' was replaced by the 'Pick-em-up, pick-em-up, hot potatoes' of the Divine Office sung in English. His friends died, his children grew up, his health deteriorated. But he kept on working. He had written two books between *Officers and Gentlemen* and *Unconditional Surrender*, the official biography of Ronald Knox (1959) and a last travel book, *A Tourist in Africa* (1960). In 1963 he published privately his last short story, *Basil Seal Rides Again*, and in 1964, *A Little Learning*, the first volume of his autobiography. In fifteen years, between 1950 and 1964, he had written nine full-length books, as well as numerous shorter pieces.

Basil Seal Rides Again takes a mordant farewell of the Metroland characters. Peter Pastmaster flourishes; Ambrose Silk is given the Order of Merit. Margot, withered and lonely, spends her days watching television in a darkened room. The story, such as it is, has Basil preventing his daughter's marriage by pretending to have fathered her allegedly unsuitable fiancé. *A Little Learning* is beautifully crafted, at once self-revealing and cleverly self-protective, but Waugh could not get going with the second volume, which was to have dealt with his first marriage. Church affairs upset him deeply. 'The Vatican Council has knocked the guts out of me,' he wrote (*Letters*, p. 638); he clung 'to the Faith doggedly without joy' (*Letters*, p. 639). He died on Easter Sunday 1966, after hearing Mass in the old rite. Like Virginia Crouchback, he was not tried beyond his powers.

He must be counted among the great novelists of the century. He had a great and stylish comic gift, a subtle and intelligent sense of design, and a brilliantly mischievous awareness of his audience which kept him in contact with a world from which in other respects he was thoroughly estranged. His other great resource was his religion. Only the Catholic Church, in his experience, could satisfy, in Knox's words, 'the instinct for beauty, the instinct for history, the instinct for world-wide citizenship, the instinct for moral guidance, the instinct for intellectual definiteness' (*The Belief of Catholics*, p. 37) which so possessed him, and without which he would have been unable to confront the Evil in the world and in his own heart.

The two most important items in this list are the instincts for history and for intellectual definiteness. As Central Europe rises once more from the ashes of 'Eastern Europe' during the pontificate of a former Cardinal Archbishop of Krakow, Waugh's vision of history may seem less eccentric than it once did. He was a conservative but not a reactionary, at least in so far as the reactionary bands together with others to put history into reverse. He had far too independent a mind for that, and far too keen a sense of the absurd. This too may be marked up to his religion. He would rather leave things to God. In any case not many of today's Conservative-voting shareholders in public utilities are likely to be sympathetic with Mr Pinfold's medieval boast that he 'had never in his life put out a penny at interest' (p. 132). Waugh was not a man to make common cause with what passes for conservatism in the twentieth century. His idiosyncratic gifts, susceptibilities and perspectives, his fine but somewhat slothful intellect, his contempt, alarm, anger, compassion and vulnerability, made him unusually sensitive to the contradictions of his times; in consequence he and the age he lived in are vividly present in his work. His novels are uniquely valuable as a record and criticism of succeeding fashions in folly and vice, written over thirty years in one clear and characteristic fist.

Bibliography

By Evelyn Waugh

Rossetti, His Life and Works, Duckworth, 1928.

Decline and Fall, Chapman and Hall, 1928; Penguin Books, 1937.

Vile Bodies, Chapman and Hall, 1930; Penguin Books, 1938.

Labels, A Mediterranean Journey, Duckworth, 1930.

Remote People, Duckworth, 1931.

Black Mischief, Chapman and Hall, 1932; Penguin Books, 1938.

Ninety-Two Days, The Account of a Tropical Journey Through British Guiana and Part of Brazil, Duckworth, 1934.

A Handful of Dust, Chapman and Hall, 1934; Penguin Books, 1951.

Edmund Campion: Jesuit and Martyr, Longman, 1935; Second Edition with Preface, Hollis and Carter, 1947; Penguin Books, 1953.

Waugh in Abyssinia, Longman, Green & Co., 1936.

Scoop: A Novel About Journalists, Chapman and Hall, 1938; Penguin Books, 1943.

Robbery Under Law: The Mexican Object-Lesson, Chapman and Hall, 1939.

Put Out More Flags, Chapman and Hall, 1942; Penguin Books, 1943.

Brideshead Revisited: The Sacred and Profane Memories of Captain Charles Ryder, Chapman and Hall, 1945; Penguin Books, 1951; Revised Uniform Edition with Preface, Chapman and Hall, 1960; Penguin Books, 1962.

Scott-King's Modern Europe, Chapman and Hall, 1947; see below.

The Loved One, Chapman and Hall, 1948; Penguin Books, 1951.

Work Suspended and Other Stories Written Before the Second World War, Chapman and Hall, 1949; Penguin Books, 1951 (including 'Cruise', 'An Englishman's Home', 'Scott-King's Modern Europe' and [1967 edition] 'Basil Seal Rides Again').

Helena, Chapman and Hall, 1950; Penguin Books, 1963.

Men at Arms, Chapman and Hall, 1952; Penguin Books, 1964.

Love Among the Ruins: A Romance of the Near Future, Chapman and Hall, 1953; see below.

Tactical Exercise (short stories), Boston: Little, Brown, 1954; see below.

Officers and Gentlemen, Chapman and Hall, 1955; Penguin Books, 1964.

The Ordeal of Gilbert Pinfold: A Conversation Piece, Chapman and Hall, 1957; Penguin Books, 1962 (with 'Tactical Exercise' and 'Love Among the Ruins').

The Life of the Right Reverend Ronald Knox, Chapman and Hall, 1959.

A Tourist in Africa, Chapman and Hall, 1960.

Unconditional Surrender, Chapman and Hall, 1961; Penguin Books, 1964.

Basil Seal Rides Again or The Rake's Regress, Chapman and Hall, 1963; see above.

A Little Learning. The First Volume of an Autobiography, Chapman and Hall, 1964; Penguin Books, 1983.

Sword of Honour. A Final Version of the Novels: Men at Arms (1952), Officers and Gentlemen (1955) and Unconditional Surrender (1961), Chapman and Hall, 1965.

The Letters of Evelyn Waugh, edited by Mark Amory, Weidenfeld and Nicolson, 1980; Penguin Books, 1982.

The Diaries of Evelyn Waugh, edited by Michael Davie, Weidenfeld and Nicolson, 1976.

The Essays, Articles and Reviews of Evelyn Waugh, edited by Donat Gallagher, Methuen, 1983.

By other authors

Georges Bataille, *Literature and Evil*, Translated by Alastair Hamilton, Calder and Boyar, 1973.

John Dryden, *The Poems and Fables*, edited by James Kinsley, Oxford University Press, 1962.

Julian Jebb, *Writers at Work. The Paris Review Interviews*, Third Series, Secker & Warburg, 1968.

Rudyard Kipling, *Life's Handicap*, Macmillan, 1891; St Martin's Library edn., 1964.

—, *The Day's Work*, Macmillan, 1898; St Martin's Library edn., 1964.

Ronald Knox, *The Belief of Catholics*, Ernest Benn, 1927.

—, *God and the Atom*, Sheed and Ward, 1945.

John Henry Newman, *An Essay in Aid of A Grammar of Assent*, 1870; Longmans, Green and Co., 1924.

—, *Parochial and Plain Sermons*, vol. VI, 1868, Westminster, Maryland, 1967.

George Orwell, *Collected Essays*, Mercury Books, 1961.

Walter Pater, *The Renaissance. Studies in Art and Poetry*, Macmillan, 1873; Fontana/Collins, 1961.

Martin Stannard (ed.), *Evelyn Waugh: The Critical Heritage*, Routledge & Kegan Paul, 1984.

—, *Evelyn Waugh: The Early Years 1903–1939*, New York: W. W. Norton and Company, 1987.

Roderick Strange, *Newman and the Gospel of Christ*, Oxford University Press, 1981.

Acknowledgements

For permission to quote from copyright material grateful acknowledgement is made to the following:

Peters Fraser and Dunlop Group for quotations from Evelyn Waugh: *Decline and Fall*, Chapman and Hall, 1928; *Vile Bodies*, Chapman and Hall, 1930; *Labels, A Mediterranean Journey*, Duckworth, 1930; *Remote People*, Duckworth, 1931; *Black Mischief*, Chapman and Hall, 1932; *A Handful of Dust*, Chapman and Hall, 1934; *Edmund Campion: Jesuit and Martyr*, Longmans, 1935. *Scoop*, Chapman and Hall, 1938; *Robbery Under Law: The Mexican Object-Lesson*, Chapman and Hall, 1939; *Put Out More Flags*, Chapman and Hall, 1942; *Brideshead Revisited: The Sacred and Profane Memories of Captain Charles Ryder*, Chapman and Hall, 1945; *The Loved One*, Chapman and Hall, 1948; *Work Suspended and Other Stories Written Before the Second World War*, Chapman and Hall, 1949; *Tactical Exercise*, Chapman and Hall; *Love Among the Ruins*, Chapman and Hall, 1953; *The Ordeal of Gilbert Pinfold: A Conversation Piece*, Chapman and Hall, 1957; *Men at Arms*, Chapman and Hall, 1952; *Officers and Gentlemen*, Chapman and Hall, 1955; *Unconditional Surrender*, Chapman and Hall, 1961;

Quotations from R. A. Knox, *The Belief of Catholics*, 1927, are reprinted by permission of A. and C. Black; from George Bataille, *Literature and Evil*, 1973, by permission of Marion Boyars Publishers, London, New York; from T. S. Eliot, *The Waste Land*, reprinted from *Collected Poems 1909–62*, Faber and Faber Ltd, 1922, by courtesy of Mrs Valerie Eliot; from George Orwell,

Collected Essays, Secker and Warburg, 1961, by permission of A. M. Heath and Co. Ltd. and the estate of the late Sonia Brownell Orwell and Martin Secker and Warburg Ltd.

Index

Black Hat Books
2831 NE MLK Blvd
Portland